PRAISE FOR DONNA GRANT'S
BEST-SELLING ROMANCE NOVELS

"Grant's ability to quickly convey complicated backstory makes this jam-packed love story accessible even to new or periodic readers." - *Publisher's Weekly*

"Donna Grant has given the paranormal genre a burst of fresh air…" – *San Francisco Book Review*

"The premise is dramatic and heartbreaking; the characters are colorful and engaging; the romance is spirited and seductive." – *The Reading Cafe*

"The central romance, fueled by a hostage drama, plays out in glorious detail against a backdrop of multiple ongoing issues in the "Dark Kings" books. This seemingly penultimate installment creates a nice segue to a climactic end." – *Library Journal*

"…intense romance amid the growing war between the Dragons and the Dark Fae is scorching hot." – *Booklist*

DON'T MISS THESE OTHER NOVELS
BY NYT & USA TODAY BESTSELLING AUTHOR
DONNA GRANT

CONTEMPORARY PARANORMAL

DRAGON KINGS® SERIES

REAPER SERIES

DARK WARRIORS SERIES

CHIASSON SERIES

ROGUES OF SCOTLAND SERIES

Book 1: The Craving

Book 2: The Hunger

Book 3: The Tempted

Book 4: The Seduced

Books 1-4: Rogues of Scotland Box Set

THE SHIELDS SERIES

Book 1: A Dark Guardian

Book 2: A Kind of Magic

Book 3: A Dark Seduction

Book 4: A Forbidden Temptation

Book 5: A Warrior's Heart

Mystic Trinity (a series connecting novel)

DRUIDS GLEN SERIES

Book 1: Highland Mist

Book 2: Highland Nights

Book 3: Highland Dawn

Book 4: Highland Fires

Book 5: Highland Magic

Mystic Trinity (a series connecting novel)

SISTERS OF MAGIC TRILOGY

Book 1: Shadow Magic

Book 2: Echoes of Magic

Book 3: Dangerous Magic

Books 1-3: Sisters of Magic Box Set

STAND ALONE BOOKS

That Cowboy of Mine

Home for a Cowboy Christmas

Mutual Desire

Forever Mine

Savage Moon

Check out Donna Grant's Online Store at

www.DonnaGrant.com/shop

for autographed books, character themed goodies, and more!

DARK ALPHA'S PASSION

REAPERS, BOOK 14

DONNA GRANT

This is a work of fiction. All of the characters, organizations, and events portrayed in this novel are either products of the author's imagination or are used fictitiously.

www.DonnaGrant.com
www.MotherofDragonsBooks.com

CHAPTER ONE

Dublin

He was fucked. There was no getting around that. Any way he looked, every idea he had, fell apart like mist that vanished with the sun.

Ruarc paused in his wandering of the streets and watched the bright streaks of red and orange in the sky. It was a beautiful sunrise. Any other day, he might have taken it as a good omen. But he knew truths now that he hadn't before. Truths that changed *everything*.

The rage inside him threatened to explode. He wanted to hurt something. No. He wanted to tear the limbs from the six individuals who had put him in this tenuous position—*the* Six. There was only one outcome for him. He didn't fear death. He dreaded everything he would leave behind.

Ruarc leaned a shoulder against a building and dropped his head into his hands. Emotion, viscous and cloying, choked him. He might feel better if he could let out a bellow, slam his fist into a wall, or…something. But he couldn't. Those who controlled whether his family lived or died watched him. One wrong move, and those he loved could be taken from him. He'd once given up everything for them. How could he let anything happen to his family now?

He lifted his head. Dublin never truly slept. No city did. The dawning of a new day sent the seedier individuals to their holes to await the night, while other opportunistic people began filling the streets. Ruarc didn't know which he found more abhorrent.

Fae milled among the mortals—Dark and Light, alike. Some Dark didn't bother hiding their red eyes or their silver-streaked black hair. In this day and age, where humans sported various hair colors and eye shades thanks to contacts, no one paid them any heed. Though mortals were unconsciously drawn to the Fae. Ruarc rarely walked amid humans without lowering his power so they didn't gather around him. Some Fae got off on having that kind of control over mortals. He never had. He found it a nuisance. It made the humans look weak. No other being reacted to the Fae the way they did. And to most Fae, who were egomaniacs, it gave them a god complex.

Ruarc didn't hate humans. But he didn't like them, either. They were simply a part of Earth. Just as the Dragon Kings were. If Ruarc had his preference, he'd be back on the Fae Realm, not having to deal with mortals *or* the Kings.

But he wasn't on the Fae Realm. He was on Earth.

"In fekking Hell," he murmured.

As the morning progressed, the tourists began filling the streets. They were oblivious to the threats walking alongside them. His gaze locked on a woman, staring at him. She had her blond hair pulled back in a ponytail that looked as if she had slept in it. For some unknown reason, mortals thought that was a good look for them. They were wrong.

She was a twenty-something in jeans, a white t-shirt, and white sneakers. It was how she stared at him that got his attention. It didn't take Ruarc long to realize that this wasn't just any human. The woman was a Druid.

But why was she staring at him?

Druids were all over the world, but the strongest of them resided on the Isle of Skye. It wasn't an oddity to find a Druid walking the streets of Dublin. What bothered him was the way she observed him. He quirked a brow, daring her to come closer. She dropped her gaze, and a heartbeat later, turned and walked away.

Ruarc almost followed her. *Almost.* In the end, he didn't care that she had been staring. So what if she knew he was Fae? Most Druids' magic had been diluted through the generations, which meant many hardly had any left. Every once in a while, one was born with significant power and had no idea what it was or how to use it. However, Ruarc had more pressing concerns than the Druids.

He turned his thoughts from the human and back to the matter at hand. The fuckery he was currently mired in. He sighed loudly. His first thought was to run far and fast. If only that were an option. His life wasn't the one on the line, though. It was his family's.

Ruarc ran a hand down his face and pushed away from the building to continue walking. He had no destination in mind. It wouldn't matter if he did. The Others would find him. They always did.

"Fek," he said as his anxiety rose.

He didn't only have the Others watching him. Now, there were the Reapers.

"Fekking Reapers," he said with a shake of his head.

He'd believed that Rordan was his friend. It had been so long since Ruarc had found someone he thought he could trust. In the end, he'd discovered that Rordan had the biggest secret of all. He was a Reaper. It explained so much about his actions on Achill Island. Rordan had been undercover. He hadn't cared a whit about anyone or anything but his mission.

Even if Ruarc wanted to turn to Rordan for help now, he couldn't chance it—not that the Reapers would help him.

Ruarc didn't look around to see if anyone followed. He knew he was being trailed. His every action scrutinized. He'd never hated anyone more than he did the Six who governed the Fae Others. They wanted power. And they didn't care who died for them to obtain it.

The sounds of the city made Ruarc tense. He needed

somewhere to sit and think. He needed quiet. He briefly thought about his flat in Dublin but decided against it. There was only one place he wanted to go.

Ruarc lengthened his strides and crossed the busy street. For the ten minutes it took him to walk to Trinity College, his thoughts receded. He entered the campus and made his way to the rose garden. The instant his feet hit the grass, he paused and closed his eyes.

It had been so very long since he had been here. He wouldn't be here now, except the location had reared from his memories, and he'd been unable to shove it aside. Ruarc slowly opened his eyes and looked around at the lush beauty of the gardens. Stately trees, numerous flowers, and of course, roses everywhere.

He scanned the area. It was quiet, the garden seemingly keeping the hum of the city back. A few humans strode about, but no one paid him any heed. He spotted three wooden benches in the garden, set in a corner with a black iron fence behind them. Ruarc chose the middle one and slowly sank onto it.

A cherry blossom tree stood before him, its branches thick with blooms, stretching out as if to touch him. He took a deep breath, letting the scents of the garden try to cleanse him, and then slowly released it. He hadn't had time to think about the full impact of what he found himself involved in. However, his thoughts didn't give him a choice now. Flashes of the Six as they surrounded him, the fear and fury he'd felt as the realization of his predicament sank in, and the sight of Rordan with the Reapers kept going through his mind.

If he called for Rordan, would he come? Ruarc didn't dare try. The Six had known what they were doing when they brought him to their compound. The Reapers had seen him there. They wouldn't trust him. He wouldn't, in their shoes. But that only made his situation more difficult.

It was in his nature to find a way out of any problem. He was a problem solver. It was why everyone in his family turned to him. For a long time, he'd believed that he could handle things on his own.

Now, he realized how foolish he'd been. Even before the Six, he was the only one who'd had anything to lose in his family. He had put everything on the line for them.

His family went about their lives as if nothing had changed. All the while, he did everything he could to repay his father's debts and square the favors called in and continued to make money to support the way of life that everyone in his family was accustomed to. He should've washed his hands of all of them.

But that wasn't what a good son did.

Never mind that a good father never would've put his family in such a predicament or placed everything on his son's shoulders. His father had already done his misdeeds, and Ruarc had stepped in— as expected—to save the family. It was no use thinking of all of that now. What was done, was done. He'd made his choices. There was no going back now.

All these centuries, he'd thought he'd been doing the right thing. Had believed his actions would prove how valuable he was to his family, and that his father might actually be proud of him. Ruarc still waited to hear those words.

When his father retreated, and Ruarc took control of things for the family, he had made a promise to himself that he would be fair in his dealings. That no matter the cost, he would pay back all the money and return every favor. Some of those had been out of Ruarc's comfort zone, but he'd honored them anyway. With each favor and cent repaid, he'd felt that he was headed in the right direction. He'd done everything right.

Or so he'd thought.

Ruarc had given up the life he wanted. The woman he loved. He'd put aside everything he wished for to take care of his family. It was expected.

Expected. His father threw that word around a lot. Ruarc had never said that he expected his father to be the man he professed to be. Maybe he should have.

None of that mattered now. Not with his current quandary. Ruarc had kept his ear to the ground, listening for news of what had

occurred on the realm, but he'd never gotten involved. His focus
had been on his family and keeping them out of trouble.

Like most Fae, he hadn't been aware of the group of beings who
called themselves the Others. They consisted of a Light and Dark
Fae, a *mie* and *drough* Druid from Earth, and a *mie* and *drough* from
another realm. Their intention was to kill the Dragon Kings and
take the planet for their own so they could have the magic. Their
combined power had done a number on the Dragon Kings. But in
the end, the Kings prevailed.

Now, the Fae had decided to create their own group of Others.
The Six who led them were comprised of three Light and three
Dark. The Light and Dark detested each other. Their realm had
been destroyed because of their civil war, sending them fleeing to
Earth. The fact that Dark and Light were willing to work together
was enough to draw Ruarc up short.

A Fae's magic was considerable. It was more powerful than any
Druid's magic—even those from the Isle of Skye. To have six
combine their power should make every soul on the realm quake in
their shoes with dread.

To make matters worse, the Six had amassed a group of Fae.
Brainwashed them to believe everything the Six said. Then there
were the soldiers. Ruarc fisted his hands that lay on his thighs. He
was strong in his own right, but those bastards had magic that
exceeded a normal Fae's. It was how they had taken him from Achill
to begin with.

Ruarc leaned forward and rested his elbows on his knees as he
gazed at the grass. A bug crawled over one blade after another,
barely making any headway. He stared at the insect as he thought
about Achill Island. He may not have liked some of the Fae who
had gathered at Moorehall, but to learn that those not chosen to
join the Others had been killed and their magic consumed by the
Six sickened Ruarc.

The Six were exceptionally powerful. In the short time he'd
been with them, he'd learned there was only one path for him—the
one *they* had chosen for him.

Yet, every fiber of his soul screamed against it.

He'd fight if there was a way.

"Hey, Ruarc."

He stiffened at the sound of Rordan's voice.

CHAPTER TWO

Chevonne refused to break eye contact with Oscar. For a short time, she'd thought he might be the man she would spend the rest of her life with. But she'd been wrong. Again.

How many times would she be wrong? But she knew the answer —*she would never be happy with the one she loved*. The thought of Ruarc made her stomach clench with need and sorrow.

"I thought we were in a good place," Oscar said as confusion lined his face. "Our two families are well thought of in the Light community. We're a power couple."

She stopped short of rolling her eyes. Oscar thought it was clever to use human sayings. She didn't. While she'd once thought it humorous, it now irritated her to the point of resentment. Everything he did grated on her nerves.

"Chevonne," he said and took a step toward her.

She immediately backed away and held up a hand. "We've said all there is to say."

"I disagree. We've spent the past decade together. We've had our ups and downs, but that's any relationship. Why do you want to throw this away? I've bent over backwards for you."

It was on the tip of her tongue to tell him all the things he'd done—or *hadn't* done—that had led to the demise of their relationship. She wanted to recount every single incident. She had kept a list in her head for a long time now. But it wouldn't be worth the effort. Oscar could be charming when he wanted. And right now, he wanted *her*. The minute she relented, he would return to how he'd acted before.

She assumed part of the blame. After all, she had let the relationship go on for far longer than it should have. She should've ended it years ago. Chevonne had known then that Oscar wanted more than she would ever be willing to give. Yet, she had tried. Maybe not with her whole heart, but she *had* given it a shot. That's what lonely people did—those who wanted to love and be loved. The problem was, she kept doing that with the wrong men.

Anger flashed in Oscar's eyes as his face contorted with disgust. "You're going to regret this. You'll come back to me within a month. Be prepared to do a lot of begging. I'm a prime catch. Literally hundreds of Fae women out there would do anything to have me."

"I hope you find the one for you," she said and turned to leave. Oscar's hand wrapped around her arm. She paused and looked down at it before lifting her gaze to his face. "Release me. Now."

"Don't go."

Was that a note of fear she heard in his voice? His fury was gone, but she didn't trust the tinge of panic he wore now. "This is for the best."

"Chevonne, please. I need you to stay. They…"

She frowned when he trailed off. "They what?"

"Nothing." He shook his head and glanced away. "Just stay. I'll be whatever you need me to be."

He was lying. Of that, she was positive. He must be speaking of his family. They had been after Oscar and Chevonne to get married for some time. She had been the one to put them off with one excuse after another. Her family was quite happy they hadn't gotten married since they hadn't been too keen on Oscar to begin with.

Chevonne gently pulled her arm from his grip. "Goodbye, Oscar."

Instead of walking out the door, she teleported away so he

wouldn't try to grab her again. She jumped to two more locations before she was able to take an easy breath. Even then, she looked around to make sure that he hadn't somehow followed her. She had never seen such a look of desperation in his eyes. Surely, he couldn't be that upset about her not attending the event with him that evening. She wasn't even sure what it was. He hadn't told her much, other than it was a special privilege to be asked.

When he refused to divulge more, she had been instantly on guard and wary of attending. Chevonne didn't like secrets or surprises. That was one reason she had ended things this morning. Her cowardice had kept her from doing it sooner—maybe because she knew what it was to be hurt in a situation like that.

It might have been many, many years since she'd had her heart broken, but the scars were still there. Same as the heartache. Her father kept telling her that until she let go of the past and the one who'd gotten away, she would never find happiness with another. She wrinkled her nose as she thought of the string of relationships she had ended since getting hurt. Her father had a point.

Chevonne walked the streets of Dublin. She liked getting lost in the crowds. The noise of the city and its occupants was like white noise. It allowed her to contemplate and think. She considered where she would go now. Remaining in Dublin, where she would most likely run into Oscar, might not be the best idea. It had been a while since she had been up north. Perhaps some time on her family's estate before deciding what her next stop would be was in order.

She turned to cross the street when something caught her attention out of the corner of her eye. She glanced to the side and caught sight of two Fae dressed in all black, standing perfectly still amid the tourists. Chevonne did a double-take, but they were gone. They had been there. She was sure of it. Just as she was positive that they had been looking at her.

A chill raced down her spine. Was this Oscar's doing? Perhaps she needed to leave Dublin sooner. Chevonne scanned the area once more, waiting for the Fae to appear in another place. Dark Fae loved to wear all black, but one of the Fae had been Light. The fact that they had been together and dressed similarly was curious.

She hurried across the street when the light flashed for her to go. The longer she walked and didn't see anything, the more she wondered if it had only been her imagination. Every time she thought about ducking out of the mortals' sight and teleporting away, something made her stay. She had no idea why until she realized where she stood.

"Trinity College," she said as her steps slowed.

She paused in front of the entrance. There wasn't a time she didn't pass by that her thoughts didn't return to the past. She wished she could let it go. The past didn't hurt quite as bad at times, but the pain never truly went away. It was always there, waiting to remind her of how happy she'd once been. Of how deeply she had loved.

And how shattered she had become when it was over.

Chevonne hadn't stepped foot in the college since. She hadn't wanted to. It was odd that something compelled her to walk through the main gates now. Hesitantly, she made her way onto campus. It felt weird to be back. So much had changed—and so much hadn't.

She loved the architecture of the older buildings. They were so grand and beautiful to behold. She hadn't attended the college. No, she had simply liked walking the grounds and buildings. Something about them made her smile. The humans might not have magic, but they could create stunning works of art in their structures.

As she strolled through the grounds, she found herself smiling again. Some students hurried from one place to another, while others stood talking in small groups. The deeper she went, the more she realized that she had missed out on so much beauty because she feared for her heart.

Feared the memories being back on the grounds would dredge up. And she was right to worry. Returning to campus stirred up everything. No, that wasn't entirely true. She had been thinking about the past, of how her life *could* have gone, for some time now. It was like it had a hold on her and refused to let go.

Or was she the one who wouldn't loosen her grip?

Chevonne turned with the path, seeing the museum ahead and

then the rose garden. She wanted to turn away from it but she couldn't. Once, so very long ago, she'd had a magical night in the garden with the love of her life.

"Ruarc," she whispered as her eyes swam with tears.

She blinked them away, but she didn't shy away from the memories. Instead, she embraced them, savoring every second that replayed in her mind. She'd discovered true happiness that night. She had known then that he was the one for her.

No matter how hard she tried to stay in that memory, it slipped away. It would be easy to remain in the past and replay the memories on repeat. It was more tempting than she would ever admit.

Chevonne sighed as her gaze skirted away. She jerked her head back. Her heart skipped a beat when she saw a man sitting on a bench. Chills raced over her skin, and she couldn't draw breath into her lungs. She knew how he held himself. The tilt of his head. Even across the distance, she knew it was Ruarc.

For an instant, she almost called out to him, but she stopped herself. The last time she had seen him, he'd torn her heart to shreds and left her standing in the rain. Her pleas and tears hadn't cracked his hardened shell.

Her hands were clammy, her heart racing now. Once, she had searched every face for his, hoping to encounter him. After a while, she became thankful that never happened. It was strange to see him now. He was a part of her life that she had desperately tried to let go of but never quite managed. Her sisters repeatedly told her it was because she was still in love with him. Eileen, her eldest sister, even mentioned trying to find him. Chevonne had nixed that idea quickly. If he didn't want her, then she wouldn't chase after him.

She couldn't take her eyes from him now. He sat forward, a frown on his face as if he were troubled. Despite how badly he had wounded her, she wanted to comfort him. Mostly, she wanted to be near him, to see his pale silver eyes and hear his deep voice.

Chevonne knew nothing of his life now. She'd done that on purpose. She didn't want to know if he was with someone—though she was sure he was. A man like Ruarc never stayed single for long. He had so many good qualities, despite his questionable family.

Now, she understood what had drawn her to Trinity College. The longer she stared at him, the harder it was to walk away. It didn't matter how much time had passed since they had last spoken, she couldn't chance an encounter. She didn't trust herself. Ruarc had believed in her when others hadn't. He had shown her how to go after what she wanted. He'd been her cheerleader, just as she had been his. Their relationship had been as perfect as one could be.

Then, it all fell apart.

She still didn't know the reason. It was the one thing that had haunted her all these years. She wanted closure. Well, she'd once wanted it. Would it do any good to know now? Did it really matter why he had ended their liaison?

"Yes," she said aloud.

It mattered. If she could get the answer, then she might finally be able to close the door on Ruarc and get on with her life as she should've done long ago.

Chevonne squared her shoulders and lifted her chin before starting toward Ruarc. She hadn't gone two steps before he suddenly rose and hurried away without looking in her direction. Her lips parted to say his name, but she didn't want to chance that he might ignore her. She had wanted to surprise him. Now, her chance was gone.

She ran to catch up with him, but she couldn't find him. Chevonne stopped and threw up her hands in frustration. She sighed and turned around, her gaze catching on two Fae in solid black. Her eyes followed them as they walked. They disappeared behind a large bush and never reappeared.

She had seen the two Fae twice now. Coincidence? Maybe, but she doubted it. She glanced at all the windows looking down at her. The Fae teleported out, and anyone could've seen them. That wasn't how the Fae normally did things.

A tremor ran down her spine for the second time. She suddenly had the distinct impression that she wasn't safe, though she couldn't imagine why. Fae were all over the city. She'd seen half a dozen walking through Trinity alone. The two in black were ominous, though. For a few months now, there had been whispers of some secret organization, but she had chalked it up to rumor. The Fae loved to spread all sorts of gossip, and it was rare for any of it to be true.

She thought about the event Oscar had wanted her to attend, and she couldn't help but wonder if it might have to do with the organization.

"Ugh. Get a hold of yourself," she muttered with a roll of her eyes. "There is no secret organization."

CHAPTER THREE

Ruarc eyed the bench he was on but didn't see Rordan. When he didn't see anyone, he turned his head to look at the other benches, and then around him.

"You can't see me," Rordan said.

Ruarc slowly released a breath. Anger and bitterness burned through him. Though along with those emotions, the slimmest shred of hope appeared. "What do you want?"

"I want to know what's going on."

Ruarc snorted. "Why don't you tell me?"

There was a long pause, followed by an exhale. "You're mixed up in something you shouldn't be."

That was laughable. Ruarc didn't need anyone telling him what he already knew.

"Get out," Rordan urged him. "Walk away from this group and don't look back."

"Not an option."

"I can help."

Ruarc rolled his eyes. "You mean as a Reaper?"

"I couldn't tell you."

"It doesn't matter," Ruarc said as he straightened in his seat.

"It does. I looked everywhere for you when you went missing. The last place I ever expected to see you was with the Others."

Ruarc shrugged. "Things change."

"They're killing Fae."

Ruarc didn't reply. There was no need.

"Shite. You know, then?" Rordan asked, disbelief coloring his words.

Unfortunately, Ruarc knew more than he wanted to about the Others. He wished he never would've accepted the invite on Achill Island. Maybe then he wouldn't have caught someone's attention.

"Soldiers are here," Rordan said in a soft voice. "I can get you away. Take you somewhere we can speak privately."

Ruarc fisted his hands. "No."

"Let me help."

He hesitated. Ruarc could imagine the Six smiling maniacally if they were here. This scenario was exactly what they sought of him. For him to lure Rordan and the Reapers into a situation so the Six could kill them all. It went against everything Ruarc was. But if he wanted his family to live, he didn't have a choice.

"Ruarc," Rordan urged.

Finally, Ruarc rose to his feet.

That seemed to pacify Rordan because he said, "Follow the fence line until I tell you to stop."

Ruarc's gut knotted painfully. He thought of Rordan as a friend. They had trusted each other when there was no one to depend on. It was the first time in eons that Ruarc had relied on another. And he was about to destroy that friendship in the most brutal way imaginable.

He followed Rordan's instructions. Each footfall was like a dagger twisting in his heart. Ruarc had lived a good life. He'd once had a promising career and the love of a good woman. Then he'd learned how his father had pissed away their money, burned bridges with families and friends, and left everything for Ruarc to handle.

Everything he'd hoped for had evaporated that day. Including Chevonne. Once he'd learned the depths of his father's ruin, Ruarc knew he couldn't subject Chevonne to it. Had he spoken with her about it, she would've stood by his side. But he loved her too much to have her endure the things he knew were coming.

Now, he was going to lose the only friend he'd had in…well, he couldn't remember the last time he'd had someone that he called *friend*. Partly because he'd had to rebuild the trust his father had scorched, but also because he couldn't allow himself to trust anyone with his secrets.

Suddenly, someone grabbed Ruarc's arm. The next thing he knew, he was teleported to a boat at sea. He looked over to see Rordan's gaze on him, his brow furrowed. He released Ruarc and took a step back.

"No one can hear us here," Rordan said.

Ruarc looked around the yacht. "Nice boat."

"Why are you with the Others?"

"No pleasantries? Right down to business, then, I suppose."

Rordan turned his head to look out at the water and ran his fingers through his black hair. "Things went to shite fast on Achill. When Fi and I discovered you gone, I knew something had happened if you didn't answer my call."

Ruarc moved with the slight rocking of the boat. No land was visible. It was an excellent place for a private conversation. He might want to tell Rordan what had occurred, but did he dare? He'd chance it with just his life, but it went beyond him.

Rordan's head swung back to him. "What happened on Achill? Where did you go? Why didn't you come when I called?"

"Things were out of my control."

"Do you even care what happened at Moorehall?" Rordan snapped.

Ruarc held the Reaper's angry gaze. He didn't want to ask. The less he knew, the better. If only he had that option. "What happened?"

"The Fae selected for the Others left by one exit. The others were killed. Their power taken and directed to the Six."

This wasn't news. At least, he managed to keep his face impassive this time.

"Fekking hell," Rordan spat as he turned away, his hands on his hips. After a moment, he spun around and glared at him. "I thought you were someone I could trust. I thought we were friends. Is this how you treat friends?"

"We are friends."

The words came out before Ruarc could hold them in check. Now that they had been said, he couldn't take them back. And he'd just made everything that much more difficult.

Rordan stared at him for a long moment, his anger fading quickly. "What do they have on you?"

"It doesn't matter."

"What do they want of you?"

Ruarc slid his gaze away. He wanted no part of any of this. But he was neck-deep in the shite, and there was no getting out of it. He'd looked.

"Talk to me," Rordan urged.

Ruarc shook his head then walked to the stern of the yacht and sat. "Don't. Just leave it alone."

"I can help."

Ruarc barked out a laugh. "You can't."

"I couldn't tell you before that I'm a Reaper, but you learned it. You know how powerful we are."

He shook his head. "Stop asking. I won't tell you anything."

"You've already told me quite a bit. I know you aren't with them willingly. I'm betting they were the reason you disappeared from Achill. I'd also wager they're forcing you to join them. What I can't figure out is why."

"Leave it alone."

"Why? What are you afraid of? The soldiers? The Six?"

"Yes!" Ruarc bellowed as he jumped to his feet. "I am terrified of them. You want to know so bad, fine. I'm doing what I must to keep my family alive. If I don't, they'll kill them."

Rordan looked away, defeated. "Bloody hell. I knew it."

"There's nothing that can be done."

Rordan gaze jerked back to him. "Aye, there is. We can gather up your family and keep them safe. That way, you don't have to listen to the Six."

"The soldiers are hunting you and the other Reapers. You have enough to worry about."

"You're my friend."

Ruarc smiled sadly. "Why is it the Reapers keep themselves secret?"

"What does that have to do with anything?"

"You aren't the only one who can figure things out, Rordan. For instance, you couldn't tell me who you really were in case I tried to ask for a favor or special treatment."

Rordan's nostrils flared as he stared. "Things are different now."

"Are they?" Ruarc snorted. "I don't think they are. Do the other Reapers know you're here?"

Rordan once more turned his back to Ruarc. They stood in silence for long minutes before Rordan spoke. "There was a battle on Achill. Soldiers from the Others were there. Dorcha killed Fianna."

"Shite, Rordan. I'm sorry. I know you had feelings for her."

"I love her."

Ruarc noted the present tense of the word. "Fi's alive?"

"Extenuating circumstances."

"I'm happy for the both of you. I take it you two are together?"

Rordan glanced at him over his shoulder, a shadow of a smile on his lips. "Aye."

"Focus on keeping yourself and your brethren alive. The Others are coming for you, and they won't stop until all of you are dead."

Rordan faced him. "We're aware of their plans."

"Ah. Breda. I'd forgotten about her."

"The Six are now five. We killed one. We can kill the rest."

"They're Six. They'll always be Six. You can take out as many as you want. They have others waiting to take their place."

Rordan's black brows drew together. "It's our job to keep the balance with the Fae. The Others are tipping it, and we won't stand by and do nothing."

"The Six grow stronger with every Fae they kill. I know you're powerful, but I don't know if you can stand against the Others."

"We'll soon find out."

Ruarc shook his head. "The Reapers may be the only thing that stands between the annihilation of this realm and peace. Be careful. And stay away from me."

"What do they really want with you?"

"Only they know."

"Don't give me that horseshite. We created a bond on Achill. Do me the courtesy of being honest," Rordan snapped.

Ruarc swallowed. "I come from a disgraced family. I've made my living as honestly as I can, but I spend most of my time repaying my father's favors. I have no wife, no friends. Why would they want me, Rordan?"

"Me," Rordan said in a soft voice.

"The Six want me to get in contact with you and ask for your help."

"Then you'd tell them where we were so the soldiers could come for us."

"Aye."

Rordan ran a hand down his face. "I played right into their hands by coming to see you today."

"I don't plan on telling them about this conversation."

Rordan's silver eyes met his. "You may not have a choice."

"I have no wish to betray you or the other Reapers."

"The Six know you'll do exactly what they've asked because of your family. This isn't on you. They've put you in an impossible situation. Besides, you owe no loyalties to me or my brethren."

Ruarc sat down once more. "That's why I'm asking that you stay away."

"That's exactly what I'm not going to do."

The smile on Rordan's face made Ruarc frown. "What are you thinking?"

"The Six believe you're doing their bidding. That works in our favor."

When Ruarc realized what Rordan was suggesting, he shook his head. "It won't work."

"It will. The Six think they're using you, but you'll be using them and working with us."

Ruarc had been so caught up in his situation that he hadn't looked at the bigger picture. Nor had he seen that there was another way. Rordan's plan might work. To be honest, Ruarc wished he had come up with it.

"You trust me enough for this?"

Rordan grinned. "I do."

"Your brethren?"

"Let me talk to them. We'll figure it out. The Six want to ambush us. This could be a way for us to get the upper hand and squash the organization before it becomes any bigger."

For the first time, Ruarc felt that there might actually be a way out for him. "I'll be watched."

"I've been moving about among the humans and Fae for a lot longer than the soldiers. Leave them to me. I'll be in contact soon. Go about your daily life as you have been."

Ruarc shrugged. "Easy enough."

"Keep away from anyone you might know. The less you give the Others to use against you, the better."

"You don't have to worry about that."

CHAPTER FOUR

For the rest of the day and into the night, Chevonne couldn't stop thinking about Ruarc. She regretted that she hadn't called out his name. She wanted—no, she *needed*—to talk to him. She wasn't sure what she was going to say, but that didn't matter now.

It was one in the morning when she left her flat and made her way to The Stag's Head. Chevonne rarely went to the pub, but this was a special occasion. The Stag's Head sat at the corner of Dame Court and Dame Lane in the famous Temple bar district. Traditional Irish music poured from the pub as she drew close.

She barely glanced at the Victorian pub with its red Connemara marble columns. A giant, antlered stag's head hung over the entryway, greeting all who walked inside. She paused and looked at the mosaic, marble-tiled floors, granite tabletops, and mahogany bar topped with red Connemara marble. Though the stained-glass windows were one of the highlights of the pub, in her opinion.

Chevonne made her way to one of the curved booths done in button-tufted red leather. She stopped before the table where a Light Fae had his arm around a pretty female while talking to a group of Light. When Cillian looked her way, his eyes lit up.

"Cousin!" he shouted as he jumped to his feet and embraced her. He leaned back and smiled. "I'm happy to see you out."

Cillian looked behind her, scanning the crowd. "No Oscar?"

"Thank the stars."

They shared a laugh. His silver eyes studied her. "I'd like to think you missed my sterling company, but I suspect there's something else you need."

She pressed her lips together. "I need a favor."

"Anything."

Chevonne glanced at his friends, who watched the exchange with interest. She then looked at him.

"Ah," Cillian said. "Come this way."

He led her to the back of the pub where they went through a doorway to his private office. When the door closed, it shut out the noise and music. Cillian sank into the office chair and patiently waited for her to begin.

"I need you to find someone for me," she said.

"I just need a name."

Chevonne hesitated. Once she put this in motion, she couldn't take it back. Was this really what she wanted?

Cillian touched her hand, his brow furrowed as concern filled his eyes. "What's going on? Are you all right?"

"Yes," she assured him. "And you can tell the family that I ended things with Oscar this morning."

Cillian didn't bother to hide his smile. "Everyone will be pleased. He was nice enough, but he wasn't for you."

"No," she said absently, thinking of the thrill that had gone through her when she realized that she had spotted Ruarc. She didn't know how long she sank into her thoughts before she stirred herself and blinked. Only to find her cousin watching her curiously.

He grinned. "I can't do anything without a name."

"I'm trying to decide if I really want you to do it."

Cillian guided her into the other chair and turned it to face him. "Tell me the name, and let me do what I do. Once I have the information you seek, you can decide if you want to contact them."

"Have you ever been in a situation that you knew wasn't right?

Like your life was supposed to have been something else, but it got derailed? I've lived like that for so long, I was beginning to think it was normal. It isn't."

One side of his lips curved in a smile. "I think I can guess who you want me to locate."

"Is it the wrong thing to do?"

"You've never stopped loving Ruarc. I think you deserve to know the truth. He owes you that, at least."

She nodded slowly in agreement.

Cillian quirked a black brow. "Do you want a relationship with him again?"

"No. Maybe," she amended. Then sighed loudly. "I don't know."

"You need answers. Closure. You won't get that unless you talk to him. But why not just call for him?"

She shook her head adamantly. "I don't want to wait for him to decide to speak with me. I want to be the one who confronts him."

"Understandable," Cillian replied.

"You would tell me if I was doing something stupid?"

He laughed and sat back in his chair as he released her hand. "You know I would. And I expect the same from you."

"Always."

"I'll start my search immediately."

Chevonne crossed one leg over the other. "None of those at your table holding your interest tonight?"

Cillian threw back his head and laughed. "You know me too well, cousin. Entirely too well."

"Your parents want you to settle down."

"Ugh. Both of ours do. They'll keep waiting for me. I'm not jumping into anything. I'm still young."

Chevonne always felt better after talking to Cillian. She rarely came to his pub, usually only seeing him at family functions. She needed to change that. Cillian was in his element at the bar. Out of all her cousins, he was her favorite. They had always been close.

"Your smile is easier," he remarked.

She rolled her eyes. "You get all the credit."

"Damn straight, I do. If you're interested, there's a Fae out there that could take your mind off things."

Chevonne shook her head. "Not my style."

"Never has been," he said with a wink.

As much as Chevonne loved being with her cousin, the crowded pub wasn't her scene. She gave him a kiss on the cheek before he walked her out of The Stag's Head.

"I'll be in touch soon," he promised her.

She waved and returned home. Cillian had connections everywhere. She didn't know how he created them, nor was she interested to learn the particulars. Her cousin lived his own life regardless of what anyone said. She loved him for it—and envied him a bit, too. She couldn't ignore what her parents wanted and expected of her. It was too ingrained.

Cillian's parents did the same, but he ignored them. Few understood him. She had never questioned him. Maybe that's why they had remained close. In her eyes, he was the brother she'd never had. She had two sisters, and he had one brother. From her earliest memory, she and Cillian were always together during family gatherings. He always made them bearable.

She returned to her flat and turned on some jazz to fill the silence. Ruarc had introduced her to jazz. Something about the music reached right to her soul.

Chevonne changed into a heather-blue lounge set and curled up on her sofa. She leaned back, her gaze on the ceiling as she listened to the melody while her mind drifted. It wasn't long before it returned to Ruarc.

What was she going to say to him? *Should* she speak to him? Would it be better to leave things in the past and move forward?

"Right? Because I've done such a bang-up job on that so far," she said with a shake of her head.

She put her hand on her forehead and propped her elbow against the back of the off-white sofa. There was no doubt that Cillian would find Ruarc. And she didn't doubt that she would confront him. She needed the truth to move forward. Chevonne didn't want to be stuck in the same rut that she'd been in. It was time to make a new road. Ending things with Oscar and getting answers from Ruarc was the beginning of that.

A knock startled her. She jerked upright before standing and walking to the door. A look through the peephole showed it was Cillian. Worried, she hurried to move aside her wards that prevented a Fae from teleporting into her flat and opened the door.

"Hi," Cillian said with a bright smile.

"Hi."

"You going to invite me in?"

She stepped aside so he could enter and closed the door behind him. "Is something wrong?"

"Not at all." He turned and handed her a piece of paper.

Chevonne stared at it for a long moment before lifting her gaze to him. "What's that?"

"Ruarc's location."

"That was quick."

Cillian shrugged nonchalantly. "I've known where he's been for some time now. I've just been waiting for you to ask."

She looked down at the paper and worried her lip with her teeth.

"You were fearless in everything you did. Until Ruarc broke your heart. You need to find that same pluckiness again, cousin. Take the paper. Confront him. Get your answers."

"You're right. I used to be fearless." She took the paper from him.

Cillian grinned, his eyes twinkling with merriment. "I should've given you that at the pub, but I wanted an excuse to see your place."

"You don't need any pretext. Come over any time."

"Same goes for you."

"I will. Promise."

He glanced at her hand holding the address. "Want me to come with you?"

"I don't want to go alone, but I need to."

"You can do this."

She laughed. "Thanks. I owe you."

"Never," he said with a shake of his head. "You're family. But I do want to know how it turns out."

"I'll give you all the details."

"I'm holding you to that," he said with a wink.

After he left, Chevonne set the paper on her glass coffee table and stared at it. She paced the living area, sat on the couch, then paced some more. When sunlight poured through her windows, she was still staring at it.

Finally, she roused herself to take a shower. She dressed in her favorite outfit and returned to the living room. Chevonne snatched up the paper and unfolded it to reveal the address. She carefully folded it again and stuffed it into her pants pocket as she veiled herself and teleported to the location. She had a quick look around to make sure no humans saw her before dropping her veil. She hated that Fae couldn't hold veils for very long, but perhaps it was good since anyone could be standing near her while invisible.

She touched her hair to make sure everything was in place before walking to the doors of the building and directly to the lift. Inside, she punched the top floor and waited for the doors to close. Her heart pounded, her blood running like ice in her veins. She wiped her palms on her pants and tried to even her breathing. Never had she been so nervous about anything.

The lift dinged to denote the arrival of her selected floor. The doors opened, but she didn't move. There was still time to turn around and try this another day. She stood there for so long that the doors began to close.

Chevonne reached out and stopped them before finally hopping off the lift. She made her way to the door, her knees quivering so badly, she thought they might buckle. At the door, she raised her hand and saw it shaking. She drew in a deep breath to steady herself and knocked before she chickened out.

A moment later, the door opened, and she found herself looking into silver eyes ringed in black—ones she knew so well. The same thrill from the morning before went through her.

"Hi, Ruarc."

CHAPTER FIVE

The sight of Chevonne was like a dagger in Ruarc's gut. How many times had he hoped that she might seek him out? Thousands? Millions? He'd lost count through the years. He rubbed his chest over his heart as it thudded painfully against his ribs.

She wore a sexy white jumpsuit with a halter neck that dipped into a deep V to show her cleavage and hourglass figure. A wide, matching belt encircled her trim waist and showed off her luscious curves. Three gold necklaces of varying lengths hung around her neck. Through her long, straight, black locks, he spotted small gold earrings. There was more gold at her wrists and on her fingers.

There was beautiful. And then there was Chevonne. Sophisticated, elegant, and gorgeous, she personified the best of the Fae—all of which came as naturally to her as breathing.

Her oval face had impossibly high cheekbones and wide, full, kissable lips. Her large eyes were slightly elongated and held dark silver irises that regarded him with a mixture of resentment and fury. Not that he could blame her. She had every right to want his head on a platter.

Of all the times for Chevonne to find him, this was the worst.

"Nothing to say?" she replied cuttingly.

Ruarc glanced toward the lift. He had sought out Chevonne a few times to get a glimpse of her. He never stayed long because just seeing her was a temptation he shouldn't indulge. Their paths never crossed. He'd made sure of that—even if he hoped Fate would intervene.

"You look good," he told her.

She quirked a perfectly arched black brow. "May I come inside?"

"No," he said. "You shouldn't be here. Go, before it's too late."

"Too late?" she asked with a bark of laughter.

He held her gaze. "Now isn't a good time."

"I don't give a shite."

Ruarc had always been impressed with how Chevonne went after things she wanted. He had been one of them. She had made his life better in every way possible. Memories of their time together were the only things that got him through most days. Especially now.

He tried a different approach. "I'm not trying to hurt you. I'm being honest. It's danger—"

"I'm not leaving until I have what I came for."

"Chevonne, I'm begging you."

She glared at him.

Ruarc had no idea if anyone had seen her come into his building. If the Six made even a cursory look into his past, they would find Chevonne. Ruarc had done what he could to protect her from the backlash of his family's fall from grace, but he didn't know if he could help her if the Six discovered that she was here.

But she was already at his flat. The damage had been done. Being so close to her made him want to reach out and touch her. Feel her softness and have her arms wrapped around him. He would never ask it because he didn't deserve her comfort. That didn't stop him from yearning for it, though.

He stepped aside to allow her entry. Chevonne swept past him, her lavender scent slamming into him like a highspeed train. He clenched his hands to keep from reaching for her. Having her near and in his home was the worst kind of torment he could think of.

Chevonne stood in the middle of his penthouse. She looked from the hardwood floors to the many windows overlooking the city. She walked to the dark sofa and ran her hands along the back of it as she took in the rug, leather accent chairs, and side tables. Her head turned to the kitchen. She pivoted and went to the white Carrera marble waterfall island and skimmed her fingers along the top.

After she perused the kitchen, she glanced at the rectangular dark wood dining table and then turned to him. "Very masculine. It suits you."

"Would you like something to drink? Eat?"

"I'm fine, thanks. I'd rather talk."

Ruarc motioned to the living area. She took one of the chairs. He tried not to feel slighted by that. He chose the sofa and sank into it, resting his arm on the armrest. She kept her gaze on him and crossed one long leg over the other, showing off white stilettos.

"What did you want to ta—"

She interrupted him to say, "Why did you really call things off between us?"

Ruarc lowered his gaze to the rug and took a deep breath. "You know why."

"If I did, I wouldn't be here."

"It was the right thing to do."

She shifted in the chair. "How so?"

"My family—"

"Isn't you. I told you that from the very beginning."

Ruarc looked at her. "Your family didn't think that. Neither did your friends. No one expected us to last."

"No one but us," she retorted.

"All of this is in the past. Why dredge it up now?"

Her head tilted as she stared. "You refused to tell me the truth then. I deserve it now."

"You know what happened with my family."

She quirked a brow and simply stared.

Ruarc squeezed his eyes closed. What was the harm in telling her now? "You know my father's fall from grace. My family was barely respectable as it was. Then my father's lies, embezzlements, and corruption came to light. He refused to take responsibility, and his business partners and friends demanded recompense. He'd begged for tons of favors as well as borrowed money from dishonest individuals who insisted on repayment. My father went into hiding. No one knew how to find him. Not even me. Being the eldest son, the family looked to me. I had no choice but to step up and do the right thing.

"That meant finding ways to return the favors and pay back the money owed the partners and loan sharks. It was dangerous at the best of times. I could no longer hold my position in the Fae army because all of my attention was focused on keeping afloat what little my family had. My father was responsible for all of this, but my family suffered."

She gave him a curious look. "And you haven't?"

Ruarc shrugged. There was no need to answer that. His wants and desires had never come into question. "I knew if I didn't put distance between us, you would've remained by my side. You and your family would've been dragged through all of that with me. I wanted to spare you that."

"That's shite."

"What do you want me to say?" he snapped. "That I didn't think I could do any of this without you? That I needed you? Yet I knew your family would eventually step in. They were too prominent. Too important not to. That I ended it first because I never would've survived had you left me in the middle of it all?"

Ruarc rose to his feet, furious with himself for letting that come out. He raked a hand through his hair as he walked to the kitchen and braced his hands on the island. It took several deep breaths before he was calm enough to speak again. Still, he didn't face her.

"You have your answer. It's time you left."

"Did you love me?"

He looked at her over his shoulder, not bothering to hide his anger. "You know I did."

"Do you still?"

Ruarc faced the kitchen once more. He was barely holding it together. Having Chevonne in his flat was everything he wanted. Yet, it was the worst time for this. The Six had already used his family. He couldn't let them use Chevonne against him, too. "Leave. Please."

"Not until you answer me."

"There's a lot going on you don't know about. I'm the last person you should be seen with."

"Ruarc."

He jerked at the sound of her voice directly behind him. She placed a hand on his back. He felt the heat of her palm through his shirt. Ruarc squeezed his eyes closed. "Don't," he begged.

"Do you still love me?" she whispered as she moved closer.

"Yes." He couldn't hold that in. He'd loved her before he found her. And he would love her through eternity.

Her hand smoothed over his shoulder. "Then nothing else matters."

Ruarc spun around and moved away from her. "Did you not hear me? There are dangerous people out there. If they see you, they'll…" He shrugged. "I don't want to even consider what they might do. I was serious. Leave and never return."

"I've waited over three hundred years to get my answers. That's three thousand and six hundred months that I didn't have your arms around me. One hundred and nine thousand, five hundred days that I didn't hear your voice."

He stared at her, not wanting to believe her words. "Chevonne, I'm begging you."

"In case you didn't understand what I said—I love you."

This couldn't be happening. Not now, not when everything else was falling apart.

She crossed her arms over her chest. "I was hoping for a better reception."

"You aren't hearing what I've been trying to say."

"I have, and I'm telling you, I don't care. There will always be bad people around. There will always be some sort of danger or another. I've been living in a fog since we broke up. For the first time in three hundred years, I feel like I have my feet under me."

Ruarc closed his eyes. Fate was laughing at him. It was the only thing he could think of for Chevonne to come back into his life when he needed to keep his distance from everyone. He'd gotten the barest shred of hope with Rordan's plan. It was too thin for him to even hold it firmly.

And now, there was Chevonne. Beautiful, amazing, love of his life Chevonne, who had no idea what she was getting herself into. Did he tell her? Did he put her in that kind of position? Worse, what if she was part of the Others? Where did that leave him then?

"Ruarc, you're starting to worry me."

He opened his eyes to look at her. There was only one choice for him. "I want nothing more than to be with you again, but you need all the facts before you make that decision."

"Those are the words you should've said the first time."

Ruarc squeezed the bridge of his nose with his thumb and forefinger. "This is an entirely different situation."

"I'm all ears."

He dropped his hand. "You won't be so flippant about everything once I tell you."

"Quit saying shite like that and just spit it out already," she said as she leaned a hip against the island.

Ruarc glanced out the window. "After all these years, why did you seek me out now?"

"I ended a relationship I was in, and I realized that I needed closure from the past. Then I saw you."

His head whipped to her. "Saw me? When?"

"This morning, at the rose garden at Trinity College."

He rubbed the back of his neck. "Bloody hell. They were there."

"Who?" she asked, a frown marring her brow.

Ruarc swiveled his head to her. "The soldiers. They've been following me. If they saw you there, then they saw you come to my building…" He trailed off, unable to finish.

"I think you'd better start from the beginning."

A new kind of pain started in his chest. Ruarc turned away and walked to one of the windows. They would approach her, he knew it. Chevonne was smart. But the Six found a way to get who they wanted. Ruarc wouldn't let anything happen to her. He'd kill every last one of them if he had to.

CHAPTER SIX

The longer Chevonne watched Ruarc, the more worried she became. Whatever bothered him was something big. Very big, by the way he was acting.

His thick, black hair was longer than the last time she'd spoken to him and swept away from his face as if he'd been running his hands through it. He was clean-shaven, showing off his firm jaw. His silver eyes ringed with black could be as warm as a summer's day, or as frigid as the north wind.

He stood tall and confident, his broad shoulders filling out his maroon V-neck tee, while the light-colored denim of his jeans showed off his amazing butt. He'd always had a way of wearing anything and making it look good, be it casual wear or a suit.

"You might need to sit down," he warned her.

She placed her hand on the marble, letting the coolness sink into her skin. "I'm fine."

His shoulders rose and fell on a breath. "I'm sure you heard about the battle at the Light Castle."

"Of course. There isn't a Fae on this realm who doesn't know what happened. I still can't believe Usaeil stood as Queen of the Light all those centuries and was actually a Dark."

"This is about more than just Usaeil. She was involved with a group known as the Others. It began with a Druid from another realm, Moreann. When magic began waning on her realm, she went looking for another and found Earth. She is the one who first brought mortals here. It was her plan to have them infiltrate everything and eventually take down the Dragon Kings." Ruarc turned to face Chevonne then. "Moreann soon discovered just how powerful the Kings were and knew she couldn't do it alone. She met Usaeil, and the two of them struck a bargain to work in tandem to remove the Kings. Still, the two of them weren't enough. Moreann brought in a *drough* from her realm, Usaeil found a willing Light to join their ranks, and they then sought out *mie* and *drough* Druids from Earth. The six of them combined their magic and set things in motion for the Kings far back in history. Little things that the Kings didn't realize was a larger attack until it was almost too late."

"But they *did* discover it."

Ruarc nodded. "They did. And defeated the Others."

"Was this before or after the Light and Dark joined together to take out Usaeil?"

"Before."

"So, the Others were eliminated, along with their plans. That's what you're telling me."

He blew out a breath. "The two Druids from Earth ran. So did the other Fae."

"Why weren't the Druids stopped?"

"The Kings didn't feel they were a threat."

Chevonne stared at him a moment. "And the Fae? If Usaeil was the Dark, then it was a Light you're speaking of."

"I am. Brian vanished. It was thought that he was too scared to show his face."

"Do you know the real reason?"

Ruarc glanced at the floor. "He told other Fae about the Others. Soon, a new group of Others joined together."

Chevonne's concern began to grow. "Light and Dark together again?"

"Aye."

"What's their objective?"

At this question, Ruarc paused and released a long sigh. "To expose—and kill—Reapers."

"Reapers? As in the stories we were told as children to make us behave?" she asked incredulously.

He nodded, never breaking eye contact.

She swallowed as it began dawning on her what he was saying. "The Reapers are real?"

"They are. They're not quite what we were told. They're a group of Fae who reap Fae souls for Death."

Chevonne's knees threatened to buckle. She made her way back to the chair she had been in and sat heavily. She let his words sink in before raising her gaze to meet his. "You know this for a fact?"

"I know a Reaper. I've seen some of the others. I don't know how many there are, but they're stronger and faster than regular Fae."

"I see," she murmured and put a hand to her brow.

Ruarc walked to the couch and resumed his seat. "I know all of this because I was unwittingly used by a Fae who was recruiting people to join the new Others. They asked me to attend the meetings, which I did because I felt I had no choice. I met another Fae there. Rordan. He was as dubious as I was about all of it, but we developed trust between us. I didn't know at the time that he was a Reaper, undercover to determine how the Fae Others worked. The Others took me and kept me prisoner. They only brought me out when they decided it was time that I knew what was going on. They gave me a choice: I could work with them to get close to Rordan so they could send in their soldiers to kill the Reapers, or they would kill my family."

"Shite," she whispered. The tale was unbelievable, but she suspected that he wasn't finished. "These are the people you were telling me are dangerous?"

He nodded once. "They're following me. Fae in all black. They usually travel in pairs."

"A Light and a Dark," she said as her stomach dropped to her feet.

Ruarc's face went pale. "You've seen them?"

"Twice today. They seemed so out of place. I thought they were following me."

"Fek," he said as he rested his elbows on his knees and shoved his fingers into his hair. His head snapped up. "Where did you see them?"

She shrugged. "Once on the street. The second time at the rose garden."

"Fek me." Ruarc rose and began to pace. "We thought they were there for me. Now, I'm not sure. Fek."

"I didn't see you with anyone today."

"Rordan was there," he said offhandedly. Then he paused as some emotion moved over his face. He continued pacing, though it appeared as if a new worry had set in.

That's when she realized what it was. "You're wondering about my loyalties. Why I showed up today, of all days. You think I'm working with these people."

"It's possible," he said, glancing at her.

"I'm not. I've never heard of them before."

Ruarc ran his hand through his hair again. "They're everywhere. Listening to everything. Getting people to do things they normally wouldn't. Rordan is my friend. I don't have any friends. I don't want to betray him, but they didn't give me a choice."

Chevonne was about to reply when she heard Oscar say her name in her mind. She had no intention of going to Oscar. He should know that.

"Rordan has a plan," Ruarc continued. "It's a dangerous one."

Chevonne rose and walked to stand in front of him. "I'm not affiliated in any way with the Others. I swear."

"I want to believe you."

"I've never lied to you. Ever. I never will."

He started to reach for her but pulled back. "I believe you."

"Tell me how this organization works. There has to be a way to bring them down."

Ruarc shook his head. "Not really."

She listened for the next few minutes as he explained the Six, the soldiers, the recruiters, and everyone else. By the time he finished, she was beginning to wonder if they *could* be wiped away.

"You said Rordan has a plan."

Ruarc's brows lifted briefly. "The Six want to use me to get close to the Reapers for an ambush. Rordan plans to turn the tables on them."

"That's brilliant. You said the Reapers are more powerful than other Fae."

"They also have Death. She's a goddess."

Chevonne's lips parted in shock. "Death is a goddess? The Six really think they can defeat the Reapers *and* a goddess?"

"They do."

Apprehension filled her. "Can they?"

Ruarc shrugged. "I don't know. They've taken magic from so many murdered Fae. Not to mention, the Six crafted a way to force a Reaper to drop their veil."

"You say that as if the Reapers can remain veiled for as long as they want."

"They can."

She'd had more surprises today than she'd ever had at once. Chevonne licked her lips. "Will the Six be the ones to attack the Reapers, or will it be the soldiers?"

"Good question."

"It needs to be the Six."

"They never leave their compound. Or they didn't until the Reapers invaded it and fought them. They killed one of the Six, but they've already replaced her."

Chevonne looked into his eyes. "You've dealt with so much on your own. You aren't alone anymore. I'm here."

"The one place I wish you weren't," he said with a sad smile.

"You think they're going to hurt me."

"Or use you, yes. It's how they operate."

She touched his face, letting her fingers move over his cheek and jaw. "I'll stand by you no matter what. I don't care what my family or anyone else says. We were meant to be together."

Relief flickered in his eyes, but he still didn't move toward her. That didn't worry her. She knew this man. Knew him better than he knew himself. He'd been her entire world once. They had loved deeply and fiercely. It was his honor, one of the things she loved so much about him, that had caused them to miss out on so many years. But that was in the past. She had her answers. It was time to move forward with the only man who had ever been in her heart.

She closed the distance between them and smoothed her hands down his chest before laying her arms on his shoulders. Their gazes held as she leaned close and pressed her lips to his. For a heartbeat, he didn't move. Then, he had her against the wall, his body pressed against hers as he ravaged her lips until she was mindless and panting.

Her body came alive. She hadn't been heartless all these years. She had just lost the only man who could make her feel. Her blood heated in her veins as desire pooled low in her belly. She slid her fingers into Ruarc's hair and held him tightly as their kiss deepened.

He lifted her, and she wrapped her legs around his waist. The next thing she knew, they were naked on his bed. He rose on his hands and looked down at her. She smiled and smoothed her hands over his muscular chest.

"If this is a dream, I never want to wake," he said.

She tugged him down for another kiss. "It isn't a dream."

"I love you. I've always loved you. I always will."

"I love you more than you can possibly know. Nothing will keep us apart again."

"Nothing," he promised as he ground his arousal against her.

She sucked in a breath at the feel of him. There would be time enough later to spend hours kissing every inch of his body. For now, she needed him inside her.

"I know what you need," he whispered.

He shifted and guided himself to her entrance. She bit her lip as pleasure zinged through her when he ran the head of his cock over her clit. Then he pushed inside, filling her, stretching her.

"Yes," she said and pulled him closer.

His arms shook as he moved his hips slowly, inching inside her until he slid all the way in. The groan that rumbled through his chest was just what she needed to hear.

"There's only ever been you," he told her as he continued pumping his hips.

She stared into his silver eyes as the flames of desire spread rapidly. There was no more talking for her. Not when pleasure was so close.

CHAPTER SEVEN

Rational thought fled Ruarc. The only thing that mattered was the woman in his arms. It had nearly killed him to let her go. How was he to turn his back on her now? Especially when all he wanted was her in his life.

He slid in and out of her wet heat. Nothing had ever felt so good, so right. He burned with a hunger that only she could quench. Ruarc looked into her eyes as he pumped his hips faster. She locked her legs around his waist, her swollen lips parted as her breathing grew erratic. Her large breasts swayed as her pink-tipped nipples puckered.

The incredible feel of her, the hypnotic sensuality she possessed, pulled him deeper into the raging desire he'd been fighting since he opened the door. She was *everything*. His past, his present, and his future. His heart swelled with love. She had come back.

For him.

"Ruarc," she whispered as her eyes grew unfocused.

He knew that tone. She was close. He thrust deeper, harder until her body stiffened. She let out a shout as release took her, her body contracting around his cock. He didn't try to hold back his orgasm. Instead, he embraced it, pursued it. When it swept through him, the orgasm snatched his breath as pleasure surged with such intensity that time seemed to stand still.

When he was able to draw breath to his lungs, he looked at Chevonne to see her still breathing heavily. Her lids fluttered open, and she smiled.

"I've missed this," she said.

He grinned and bent to place a kiss upon her lips. "Me, too."

Ruarc pulled out of her and moved to lay on the bed facing her. She rolled to him as they shared another smile. Chevonne reached for him, kissing him again and again. He sighed when she threaded her fingers into his hair, sending a shudder of contentment through him. Her touch had always soothed him, calmed him when he was most explosive.

"I can't believe you're here," he told her.

Her silver eyes held his. "I meant it earlier. I'm not going anywhere."

Ruarc looked away. "I wish you hadn't brought that up."

"Why? It needs to be discussed."

He took her hand and brought it to his lips to kiss the backs of her fingers as he met her gaze. "You don't know what you're getting mixed up in."

"You said Rordan had a plan. They're Reapers. Which, shite, I can't believe they're real."

Ruarc couldn't help but chuckle.

"Do they look different? Tell me about the Reapers."

"They look like us. Light and Dark. They're just exceedingly powerful."

"Seems to me that the Six should be worried, not the other way around."

Ruarc twisted his lips. "The Reapers don't want to underestimate the Six or their soldiers. I can attest to the soldiers' strength and power. It's far more than a normal Fae should have."

"Did the Six give them more magic like Death did with the Reapers?"

"That's my thought. Think of all the Fae who were deemed unworthy of joining the Others. The soldiers killed them, and the

Six took all that power. Why wouldn't they share some of it with the soldiers to make them more lethal? It's a sound battle plan."

Chevonne frowned. "I still don't understand the motives of this group. They want Fae to join, but they only select a few. Surely, others are finding out what's going on."

"Who's going to say anything? The ones who are asked to join believe they've been chosen and that the others are lacking. They don't go searching for them to ask questions."

She wrinkled her nose. "Families are missing members. Someone will begin speaking out eventually."

"They'll be silenced. I have no doubt."

"This information needs to get out to all Fae so they don't join. If they knew, they wouldn't be interested."

"Are you sure? This isn't our realm. We're here simply because the Dragon Kings allow it. The moment we step out of line, they'll throw us out." He snorted. "I know I would."

She gave him a flat look. "Again, my point. Don't the Fae Others realize they'll have to contend with the Kings?"

"If they can take out the Reapers and Death, then they won't fear the Dragon Kings. They want the entire realm."

Chevonne rose on her elbow. "The original Others didn't stand a chance. How do these Fae Others think they will? The Kings are going to win, and then where will we go? We were lucky to find Earth. Even then, the Dark nearly cost us this place."

He rolled onto his back and pulled her down to his chest as he wrapped his arms around her. "I don't have any answers. I feel like I'm caught in a spider's web, and there's no way out for me."

"There is. Rordan has a plan. And I'm here."

Ruarc smiled and kissed the top of her head. "I'm glad you are, but I'm also worried."

"I'm not."

He inwardly shook his head at her declaration. This was the Chevonne he remembered. Unafraid, unwavering, and steadfast. It gave her an advantage to most, but her association with him would put her in a perilous situation. "The Six will use your family against you. Believe me, they aren't joking about wiping everyone out. Do you want to be responsible for the death of everyone in your family?"

She sighed. "You know I don't."

"That's why I said it's better if you don't tangle with them."

"If you're being watched, it's too late anyway. They've seen me."

He squeezed his eyes shut. "I'm aware."

"Then we should plan." She shifted her head to look at him.

Ruarc opened his eyes to meet hers. "You're entirely too stubborn for your own good."

"I've been told that before," she said with a grin.

His arms tightened around her. "I've met a lot of dangerous people over the last few centuries, but none compared to the Others."

"Two heads are always better than one. We lean on each other. We plan, we strategize. We prepare. That's the only way we'll triumph. I don't believe that I just happened to go to Trinity College when I haven't been back since we were last there together. I don't think it was happenstance that I walked into the garden and saw you there. We are meant to do this together."

"I can't argue with that."

A wide smile split her face. "Now that that's settled, when am I going to get to meet the Reapers?"

"I don't know," he said with a chuckle. "No one is supposed to know about them. The Six changed that. Still, I don't think they want their identities known by all."

"I'm not just anyone. I'm with you."

He squeezed her in response, but his mind was already moving in another direction. "What are your plans?"

"I already told you."

"I meant for today. Will you go back to your flat?"

"I'd rather stay with you."

Ruarc thought about the wards he had up on his penthouse. They wouldn't keep a Reaper out, and he wasn't sure they'd keep a soldier barred, either. That meant the Others could come for him and Chevonne at any time.

"Ruarc?"

He blinked when she lifted her head to look at him. "I wish I could tell you my place is safe, but nowhere is."

"What about the Six?"

"They usually send the soldiers to do their dirty work. They're vicious, cruel individuals."

She worried the corner of her lip with her teeth. "Light and Dark?"

"Aye."

"How are the Light staying Light? If they're killing as freely as a Dark, shouldn't they turn? That's what usually happens."

He shrugged and played with the ends of her black locks. "I didn't ask too many specific questions."

"You saw the Six, though?"

"I did."

"Did you know any of them?"

Ruarc paused as he remembered the middle Light who had done most of the talking. "There was one. She seemed to be not only the leader of the three Light but also the Six and the Others. I thought I recognized her."

"Have you been able to place her?"

"It's right on the fringes of my memory. Or maybe I just think I recognize her because she looks like someone I've seen before."

Chevonne raised her brows. "What does your gut tell you?"

"That I know her somehow."

"Don't worry. You'll figure it out," she said as she returned to her spot on his chest.

It had been a long time since anyone had had that kind of faith in him. Ruarc was terrified of Chevonne being with him, and the Others finding out about her. But he couldn't deny that she had restored his determination and resolve.

"I'm sorry I left," he blurted out.

She kissed his chest and caressed her hand over his washboard abdomen. "I've been angry at you for a long time. When in reality, I was angry at myself for not making you listen to me then. You closed yourself off to me."

"Self-preservation."

"I know that now. You weren't being cruel. You were thinking of me."

He nodded. "I was."

"You're an idiot, though."

His brows snapped together as he stared at the ceiling. "Excuse me?"

"I thought you knew me better than that. Your actions proved that you didn't know me or care what I thought."

"Not true. I knew you would've stayed, and it would've been trying for you."

"Did you think I couldn't handle it?"

He sighed as he rolled her onto her back and came up on his elbow to look down at her. "You're mentally and emotionally stronger than almost anyone I know. You would've handled it better than I did."

"But you still left."

"The places I had to go, the people I had to see weren't the kind you needed to be associated with. I didn't want you to see some of the things I had to do."

She stared at him for a long minute before she swallowed. "Like what?"

"Favors that my father owed were called in."

"Tell me," Chevonne urged.

Ruarc looked away. "I'm not proud of the things I've done."

"Your eyes aren't red, and you don't have silver in your hair. That tells me you didn't kill anyone."

He couldn't help but smile as he slid his gaze back to her. Chevonne's faith in him never wavered. Maybe he had been wrong to end things back then. "I didn't kill anyone, no."

"But...you did other things."

Ruarc nodded slowly. "My father put me in a position where I couldn't bargain or barter when the favors were called in. I had to do whatever was needed."

"Give me an example."

He flattened his lips. "Do you remember the MacSanlys?"

"Their middle daughter was one of my friends. The business

partnership the elder MacSanly had with others was destroyed when they learned he had been embezzling funds."

Ruarc stared at her, not saying anything.

Chevonne's eyes grew round. "He didn't embezzle, did he?"

"I had to plant documents that said he did. I'm the reason that family is living in poverty and shunned by the Fae community."

She put a hand to his cheek. "This isn't on you. I blame your father for being a coward and not stepping up to take care of his problems. I blame the ones who called in that favor. You had no choice."

"But I did. I could've refused and let my family fall into ruin."

She glanced away. "You aren't that type of man. You have always thought of others before yourself. And you always will. That's what makes you stand out above all other men. Please don't carry the guilt of your father's actions and what they caused you to do. Promise me," she insisted.

"I'll try."

"That's a start. Now, come here and kiss me. I'm not nearly done with you."

His cock thickened at her words, eager to be back inside her once more. Ruarc palmed her breast and massaged it before rolling a nipple between his fingers. She gasped in pleasure, causing him to grin.

He had years of loving to catch up on.

CHAPTER EIGHT

Death's Realm

Rordan looked around at the other Reapers, Cael, and Death as they stood in a circle outside the white tower. Everyone seemed to be mulling over his idea.

"I like it," Eoghan said.

Bradach nodded. "It'll give us the advantage we need."

"Can we trust Ruarc?" Baylon asked. "The Others *did* get to him."

Rordan hadn't expected everyone to embrace Ruarc, but it still irritated him that one of his brethren would question him. "They forced him."

"Baylon has a point," Daire said.

Cael quirked a black brow. "And what is that?"

"Rordan only knew Ruarc for a short time. What if the Others were able to brainwash him to their ways, and he's the trap for us?"

Fintan tied back his long, white hair. "Fair point."

"I trust Ruarc," Rordan stated again.

Cathal widened his stance. "We didn't get to know Ruarc as you did."

"What we know is that the Six want us dead," Talin replied.

At his words, Neve shared a glance with her husband and then snorted. "Exactly. We've been searching for them, just as they're searching for us. Rordan and Ruarc's plan would give us the advantage we need to wipe out the Six once and for all."

"More will take their place. That's how the system is set up," Torin said.

Fianna nodded her head of straight, black hair. "They most likely replaced the member of the Six that we killed."

"I agree with Rordan. It's a good place to start," Kyran said.

Balladyn crossed his arms over his chest. "The smart thing to do would be to go through with this plan. But just like with our last mission, we split up. That way, if it is a trap, they won't have all of us."

"I'm not waiting this time," Fintan stated. "I go in first."

Every eye then turned to Death—or Erith as she was known to her friends. The decision ultimately landed with her. Whatever she said, went. But Erith was fair. She liked to listen to her Reapers and take their words into consideration before coming to any conclusions.

She might be a petite goddess with lavender eyes and blue-black hair, but she was unbelievably powerful. When Rordan first met her, she had worn elaborate, black ball gowns that occasionally had hints of color somewhere. She had traded those in for a mix of armor, leather, and chainmail. It suited her.

"We take this opportunity," she told them. "But we plan to be betrayed. I don't want those soldiers getting their hands on any of you."

Dubhan asked, "What of Aisling?"

There was a pause as Erith and Cael exchanged a look before Death said, "I won't call Aisling back. She must keep to the path she's on."

"I wish she could be with us," Rordan said.

Torin nodded as he looked his way. "We all do."

Aisling had been the first female Reaper—and some might say, the most lethal of them all. Rordan wasn't happy that she'd left to track down Xaneth. Not that he didn't think the royal Light Fae was worth it, but he worried that Aisling would find herself in the middle of something she couldn't get out of.

She was part of their family. They counted on each other. Trusted one another. The fact that she had gone off on her own worried all of them—even Erith. Rordan wanted to ask Death why she hadn't forced Aisling to return. In the end, Rordan recognized that Erith must know something they didn't.

Cael's purple eyes caught his. The once-Fae was now so much more. An enemy had used him to get to Erith, except Cael managed to use her magic to save himself, thereby becoming a god. Thankfully, he and Erith had finally admitted their love for each other.

"Notify Ruarc, but don't tell him everything," Cael said.

Rordan frowned. He didn't argue, though. "In case he means to betray us."

"It's the smart move," Balladyn said.

Rordan nodded at the former King of the Dark in agreement. "What of his family?"

"A couple of us can watch them," Daire offered.

Fintan shook his head, his red-ringed white eyes narrowed. "We're already down one Reaper. And we intend to split our two groups again. The last thing we need is to have that number decreased more."

"I agree," Erith said.

Rordan glanced at the ground. "Ruarc is doing all of this to save his family. If I can't promise their safety, he might not agree."

"There could be another way," Cathal said.

Erith quirked a slim, black brow. "Druids?"

"Sorcha's cousin leads the Skye Druids. I think Rhona would help," Cathal answered.

Dubhan pulled a face. "Don't forget the Druids are putting together their own Others."

"If we show them that we won't tolerate it from our kind, that might make them rethink things," Baylon suggested.

Cael looked at Erith and shrugged. "We either ask the Druids or the Kings."

"Because the Druids have ulterior motives, my vote is for the Dragon Kings," Eoghan said.

Erith sighed as she put her hands on her hips. "Con and Rhi are on Zora, getting to know their children. There's something going on there, but I've been too focused on things here to find out what. Now isn't the time to pull the Kings' attention away from whatever they're immersed in when we have other options."

"Shall I have Sorcha contact her cousin?" Cathal asked.

Death held up a hand. "Yes, but they won't be alone."

The group was silent as they waited.

Neve rolled her eyes. "She's talking about me, Fi, and the other mates."

Rordan's gaze slid to Erith to find her watching him. She studied him for a long time before asking, "Why do you look surprised? Fi and Neve were both betrayed and killed. I gave them a second chance, just as I gave to all of you. They are Reapers. It's why they're in this circle."

"I swear, Rordan, if you tell me it isn't safe to be out there, you'll be sleeping elsewhere for the next hundred years," Fianna stated, her silver eyes shooting daggers.

Rordan swallowed, caught in a difficult position. He knew Fi was one of them, just as Neve was, but he also remembered when he'd held her lifeless body, and the desolation that had consumed him.

"They remain on this realm to protect the other mates and little Breac when the rest of us leave," Cael said.

Talin gave Neve a tight smile. "I know how capable you are, sweetheart."

"They aren't the only ones," Balladyn said with a sly smile. "Every one of your mates, be they Halflings or Fae, are more than capable. They put up with all of your shite."

Bradach ran a hand down his face. "I certainly know Maeve can handle herself."

"And Catriona," Fintan said with a proud smile.

Erith looked at Rordan. "Speak to Ruarc. Balladyn, go with him as a lookout. Remain veiled. Both of you return quickly. We have planning to do."

Rordan looked to Balladyn, and the two walked toward the Fae doorway that led to Earth. Once through it, they veiled themselves and teleported to the roof of Ruarc's penthouse. They looked across to the other buildings but didn't see any soldiers.

"They could be veiled," Balladyn said.

Rordan shook his head. "Fekkers like to be seen."

"True. They're rather full of themselves."

"Let's hope they aren't waiting for us at Ruarc's."

Balladyn grinned. "I wouldn't mind a little skirmish."

"You and me both, brother," Rordan said with a laugh.

They jumped to Ruarc's flat. The wards made it a little difficult, but nothing a Reaper couldn't get through. It was quiet except for some sounds from the bedroom. Rordan looked at Balladyn, who waved his hands, letting Rordan know he wasn't going to interrupt.

After he and Balladyn had checked the rest of the flat to ensure no soldiers were waiting, Rordan dropped his veil and cleared his throat. A minute passed without anything. Rordan cleared his throat louder and then called Ruarc's name.

An instant later, the Fae came rushing barefoot from the bedroom with only a pair of jeans on, and his hair mussed. "Rordan?" he asked incredulously.

"I did say I'd return."

"Time must have gotten away from me."

Rordan glanced toward the room. "Is this a bad time?"

Ruarc shook his head quickly. "It's Chevonne. You asked me on Achill if I had a woman. I did once. I ended things with her when all the shite with my father happened. She came back into my life."

"Today?" Rordan asked skeptically.

A beautiful, tall Light walked from the bedroom, completely dressed. "Yes, today. And before you ask, I'm not working with the Others. I'll be happy to prove it to you. Fate brought me back to Ruarc, and I'm glad for it."

Rordan looked between the two. He wanted to believe her, but it was too coincidental.

"I know what you're thinking," Ruarc said. "I thought the same. The soldiers we saw in the park weren't for me. I think they were following Chevonne. She said she saw them twice today."

"They may have been her escort," Rordan said.

Chevonne came even with Ruarc. "Like I told you, I'll be happy to prove my loyalty in any way you see fit."

"Don't ask her to leave," Ruarc said. "I'll only tell her everything when she returns. Besides, the Others are monitoring me. They know about her by now. I don't want her to leave my sight."

Rordan ran a hand down his face. This was fucked up. He glanced at Balladyn, who shrugged, telling Rordan it was his call. They had one chance to get ahead of the Others. One. They'd almost had them the last time, but the Six had vanished before they could do any real harm. Even with this plan, it would be the soldiers who came. Unless…

"All right," Rordan said.

Relief filled Chevonne's face. "Thank you. I will prove that I stand with Ruarc."

Rordan bowed his head to her. "I'm Rordan."

"It's a pleasure to meet you. I'm Chevonne."

Ruarc caught his eye. "Tell me you have good news."

"I do."

"The Reapers are going to help?" Chevonne asked excitedly.

Rordan expected that Ruarc had told her who and what he was, but it was still a shock for someone to know. After so many millennia of keeping his identity a secret, he wasn't sure he liked everyone knowing. If the Six had their way, every Fae would know about the Reapers. After the last encounter with the Others, Rordan suspected not many Fae *didn't* know the Reapers were no longer a myth.

"She won't tell anyone who you are," Ruarc said.

Rordan realized that he was frowning and wiped it from his face. "It's hard to adjust."

"What would happen if a Fae did find out?" Chevonne asked.

Rordan released a breath and shrugged. "They were killed."

"I see," she said in a soft whisper.

Ruarc's brows snapped together. "How did the Six find out?"

"That's something we'd like to know," Rordan said.

Ruarc crossed his arms over his chest. "The instant the Six think I'm going against them, they'll attack my family."

"Your family will be watched. If any soldier shows up, they'll be dealt with."

"Thank you," Ruarc said, then blew out a long breath. "Where do we begin?"

Rordan looked between Chevonne and Ruarc. "We're sorting out the details. I'll be in touch soon."

CHAPTER NINE

Chevonne blew out a breath and looked at Ruarc after Rordan had teleported away. "He's intense."

"That he is," Ruarc replied with a chuckle.

"Do you feel better now that the Reapers are on board?"

"A little. There's still so much that can go wrong, though."

She shrugged and walked to him, placing her hands on his bare chest. "That could be said about anything."

"True."

She searched his gaze. "You think I'm being flippant about all of this."

"In a way," he replied. "You've not seen what the Others are capable of. You haven't been face-to-face with them."

"That's true, but I'm taking your words to heart."

Ruarc sighed and reached for her hands, clasping them between them. "You've not witnessed the darker side of the Fae. You've not seen the evil that lurks there."

"I've seen the wicked side of humans."

"It's different, sweetheart. Mortals can be malicious and evil, but not in the same way a Fae can."

"You mean Dark Fae," she corrected.

Ruarc shook his head. "I mean all Fae. Just because someone is Light, doesn't mean they don't have evil within them."

"I'm not a child. I know that everyone has some good and evil. We choose which one we nourish the most."

His gaze skated away for a moment. "I want you to be prepared. You're kindhearted, and that could cause you all kinds of problems with the Others."

"You don't think I can take care of myself." She gave him a flat stare. "I may not have been in the Light army like you, but my sisters and I were trained. I know how to defend myself with my sword, my wits, and my magic."

A slow smile spread over his face. "Do you know your eyes sparkle when you get irritated?"

"Don't try to sweet-talk me now," she stated and attempted to tug her hands free, but he held fast.

His grin vanished as his grip tightened. "Von, these people are more dangerous than anyone you've ever encountered. They kill indiscriminately. They won't care who your family is or what connections they have. They want power, and they intend to get it by any means necessary."

"I understood that when you first told me. I may not have come across any unsavory Fae, but that doesn't mean I'm blind to their existence."

"I just want you to be careful."

She wrapped her arms around him and held him close as she looked out the window behind him. His concern and fear were obvious, and she felt them, as well. Her words were meant to calm Ruarc *and* herself. Because, truth be told, she was terrified of the Fae he'd described. She had no idea how to react if one approached her or what to do, but she would have to figure it out quickly. "I want the same for you."

"I don't think that's possible with the plan taking shape."

She turned her head slightly and kissed his neck before pulling back. "We can do this. Believe it, and it will be so."

He flashed her a smile. "I will."

"What happens now? I mean after our visit from R—"

"Don't," he said over her. "Don't say his name. I don't trust that we aren't being watched. Unless my friends are here, don't mention them."

She licked her lips nervously. Chevonne hated to admit it, but Ruarc was right. She had never been immersed in anything like this before. The worst thing she'd had to endure was an evening at the Light Castle for a ball. Politics and backstabbing were par for the course at the castle—and even some of her social situations. While that could be treacherous, it wasn't anything like the dodginess Ruarc described.

Chevonne was glad that her parents had insisted she and her sisters know how to defend themselves. She'd never thought to use any of those lessons, but in light of the new information, that could change.

"What do we do? Wait?" she asked.

Ruarc shrugged, his lips twisting. "That's all we can do."

"I'm certainly not complaining. I like the idea of spending some quality time with you. We have a lot of making up to do," she informed him.

"We were interrupted."

She smiled as he tugged her close and placed his lips on hers. "Yes, we were."

Ruarc deepened the kiss. Chevonne sank against him as desire surged through her. He teleported them to the sofa, where he lay on top of her. She was about to use her magic to remove their clothes when she heard her sister call her name.

"What is it?" Ruarc asked as he pushed up to look down at her.

"Eileen is calling for me."

His brows snapped together. "Ignore her."

"Seriously? It's my sister. I can't ignore her. Either of them."

Ruarc moved off her to stand.

She slowly sat, watching him. She had forgotten about her family in all of this. They needed to know about the Others and the threat they posed. They needed to be prepared if anyone tried to recruit them. "I want to tell my family."

"No," Ruarc said and snapped his head to her.

"Why? Shouldn't I warn them? Shouldn't every Fae be told?"

He squeezed his eyes closed as a muscle ticked in his jaw. When he opened his eyes again, his anger was gone. "You're right. I'm sorry."

"Don't apologize," she said as she rose and walked to him. "You've been threatened and coerced. You're in defense mode, as anyone would be."

"I'm not going to come out of this alive."

His words stopped her cold. A shiver of dread rushed through her. "What?"

"From the moment I stood in front of the Six, I've had a feeling in the pit of my stomach."

"The Re—" She stopped herself in time. "Your friends will help. I'll help. Lest you forget, I know just how lethal you are. You moved quickly through the ranks of the Light army with your skills. The Six, the soldiers, any of the Others, they won't get their hands on you. If any of them are stupid enough to try, you will take care of them."

"You have such faith in me."

Chevonne smiled at him, but it didn't erase the churn of cold dread inside her. "I always did. And I always will."

"If something should happen to me—" he began.

She shook her head. "Don't talk like that."

"I have to. I'm going to hope for the best but plan for the worst. It's how I work."

Chevonne knew that, but she didn't want to talk about a world without him in it. Not after clearing the past with him and starting over. Yet, it wasn't fair for her to silence him. He had things he needed to say, and as much as she didn't want to hear them, she would because she loved him. She nodded for him to continue.

"All of my affairs are in order. I've kept them like that for some time now. You'll find anything you need at the cottage."

Tears filled her eyes at the mention of the cottage on the northwestern coast of Ireland. It had been their private getaway, a place where the outside world couldn't touch them. "You kept it?"

"Of course."

She hastily blinked the tears away and focused on him. Now wasn't the time to give in to emotion.

"If you find yourself in danger, call to my friend. He'll answer," Ruarc said.

"I just found you again. I don't want to talk about any of this."

His face softened. "I don't either, but we must. I have no idea when things will happen."

Chevonne winced when Eileen shouted her name. "Ugh. I need to see what my sister wants."

"Or you can call her," he said and produced a mobile phone.

She laughed as she took it. "How do you know she has a mobile?"

"Because I know you and your sisters."

Chevonne shot him an amused look as she dialed Eileen. "It's true. We do have mobiles." She halted when the line connected, and her sister answered. "Hey."

"Where are you?" Eileen demanded.

Chevonne frowned as she met Ruarc's gaze. "With a friend."

"You need to get home immediately. There's still a lot to do. I'm guessing you forgot you were in charge of the champagne."

"Bloody hell," Chevonne murmured in frustration. "I did. I'll be right there." She disconnected.

Ruarc jerked his chin to the phone. "What's going on?"

"My parents are hosting a party tonight. It starts in a few hours, and I'm supposed to be helping put the final touches on everything with my sisters."

"Can you get out of it? I don't want you to leave my side."

She rolled her eyes. "You know my family. The only way I'd get out of going was if I was dead." The joke fell flat. Chevonne stared into Ruarc's eyes and saw the apprehension filling his gaze. "Come as my guest."

"If I go, I could lead the Others to you. It's a no-win situation."

Chevonne twined her fingers with his. "I'll make a quick appearance. Then I'll return. Or, you can come with me. But I have to go. Not just because it's my family's party, but because I want to tell them what's going on with the Others. And that you and I are back together," she said with a smile.

His lips curved at the corners. "I want to be with you."

"But?"

"I don't want to bring the Six's attention to you or your family."

Chevonne blew out a breath. "I don't either, but you said it yourself. If you're being watched, then they already know about me. Therefore, they know about my family."

"I know."

"If anyone had tried to recruit someone in my family, I would've heard about it."

"That doesn't mean the Others won't," he cautioned.

She lifted one shoulder. "True. But I know what to look for. Once I inform my family, they will, too. Then, they can spread it to their friends. Whatever control the Others are taking, it's time we take it back."

"Ah, woman. I've always loved the fire in you," he whispered before kissing her.

She was breathless and thinking of ways to get out of the party when he ended the embrace. "Promise you'll always kiss me like that."

"Absolutely."

Chevonne rested her head on his chest as they held each other in silence. She didn't want to leave Ruarc's side. He was more than capable, but they weren't dealing with just any Fae. These were more powerful, which raised the stakes higher. Yet she knew they would prevail. They had to. She had endured three hundred years without Ruarc. And it had been pure Hell. She didn't want to think about him being gone forever.

"The sooner I'm gone, the sooner I can return," she said.

His arms tightened around her for a moment and then relaxed. "Call for me if there's any trouble."

"I will." She leaned back and looked at him. "I love you."

"And I you."

Fate wouldn't be so cruel as to bring them together, only to tear them apart once more. Chevonne was sure of it. She put a smile on her lips and gave him a wink. "Be back shortly."

"I'll be waiting."

She took a step back. He blew her a kiss just before she teleported away.

CHAPTER TEN

The instant Chevonne was gone, Ruarc wanted to call her back. He contemplated going to the party. He waffled back and forth before finally sinking onto the couch. It was better that he didn't go. He knew it, yet it still rankled. All he could do was pray that she remained safe and that he hadn't made a horrible decision by not going with her.

He looked around the flat. She had already left her mark after just one day. Never in his wildest dreams had he thought the love of his life would return. He wanted to shout for joy. His heart nearly burst with happiness and love.

But at the same time, his gut twisted with fear and dread. The Others would use her against him. He knew it as surely as he knew that she was the only one he would ever love.

He imagined a tumbler of whisky, and his magic produced it in his hand. Usually, Ruarc savored the smell of the liquor, but not this time. He downed it, then used magic for another. He couldn't afford to be drunk, so he savored the second drink. As he sipped the fine Irish whisky, he thought over Rordan's words.

Ruarc understood the Reaper's hesitation in trusting Chevonne. He'd had the same doubts initially, but Ruarc trusted her. If it were only his life on the line, he wouldn't care what Rordan thought. But there was much more at stake.

As if his thoughts had conjured him, Rordan suddenly appeared in the chair opposite him. Ruarc studied him for a moment. Rordan's short, black hair didn't have a strand out of place. His silver eyes were steady, watchful. In that moment, Ruarc knew that Rordan had stayed behind and listened to his and Chevonne's conversation. Ruarc couldn't even get upset since he would've done the same.

"Was it wise to let her go?" Rordan asked.

Ruarc shrugged. "You think I should've gone with her?"

Rordan held out his hand, and a tumbler of whisky appeared. "I'm glad I'm not in your shoes, brother. I'm not sure what I would've done."

"I've been second-guessing myself since she left."

Rordan lowered his gaze to the rug between them. "I'm sorry I was veiled and listening."

"You have a job to do. That doesn't mean I'm particularly happy about it."

There was a smile on Rordan's lips when he looked at Ruarc. "Understandable."

Ruarc ran a hand down his face. "If I stay, I may be letting her walk into a dangerous situation. If I go, I'll most definitely lead the Others to her."

"Damned if you do. Damned if you don't."

"Fekking sucks."

"I have to get back to the others and our planning." Rordan paused as if considering something. "Do you want me to check in on her?"

"I would be forever grateful."

Rordan downed the whisky. The tumbler vanished as he flashed Ruarc a smile. "I'll return shortly."

Once the Reaper was gone, Ruarc rose and paced. His gut twisted with worry for Chevonne. He looked out the windows, watching the sun drop into the horizon and darkness overtake the city. The past hours with Chevonne had passed in a blink. He wouldn't let them be the last he had with her.

It felt like an eternity before Rordan returned. Ruarc looked at him expectantly. "Is she safe? Tell me she's safe."

"I didn't see any soldiers. I can't say if any Others are in attendance or not. There's a lot of people there. I did see Chevonne. She's being vigilant," Rordan explained.

That made Ruarc feel marginally better. "I'm not concerned about an Other. Chevonne is skilled in combat. She can take them. I'm worried about the soldiers and the Six."

"We both discovered that the Six keep themselves hidden. You don't have to worry about them."

"A small relief."

Rordan held out his hand. The two clasped forearms.

"Thank you again," Ruarc said.

The Reaper grinned. "I'll be back with details as soon as I can."

Ruarc found himself alone in his flat once more. He used to love looking out the windows. Now, all he thought about was who might be watching him.

Chevonne loved parties, and her parents gave the best ones. The crowd was big but manageable. There were various kinds of food, soft music played in the background, and the alcohol flowed freely. Her mother could have organized the gathering in her sleep, but she liked to include her daughters. Usually, Chevonne enjoyed every part of it, but her mind was elsewhere tonight.

Before guests arrived, she'd sat her family down and quickly filled them in. To her shock, her eldest sister, Eileen, had heard of the Others. The first guests arriving had interrupted their family discussion, but there would be more talk later. Her parents had seemed shaken and concerned about the new threat. At least now, her family was aware and would know to stay away from anyone wanting to speak about the Others.

But would it be enough?

She hoped so. It'd better be. Or she would track down the

Others herself and rip them limb from limb. Her family was far
from perfect. They were pretentious and detached from a lot of
things going on in the Fae world—as well as the human one. But
they were *her* family. She bickered with her sisters, but at the end of
the day, they would fight to the death for each other.

The thought that someone might hurt them made Chevonne
look at everyone in the room differently. Because of her family and
being Light, she'd thought nothing horrendous would ever come her
way. Sadly, most Light thought that way. There was the Dark, of
course, who did their evil deeds. But that was the army's problem—
not the everyday Light.

Except, now, it looked like it was everyone's problem.

Chevonne smoothed her hands down her soft mauve dress. She
checked herself as she passed a nearby mirror. The boatneck collar
exposed one shoulder. The top was loose as it came to her waist, but
from the waist down to just below her knees, the skirt molded to her
body. She had left her hair down. She tucked a thick strand behind
an ear as she turned and surveyed the room. Anyone there could be
an Other.

Her thoughts halted when someone stepped into her line of
sight. The instant she recognized Cillian, she smiled and
hugged him.

"You wore such a frown when I walked up that I wasn't sure I
should bother you," he said when he stepped back.

She glanced away and shrugged. "Sorry. A lot on my mind."

"Does that mean things with Ruarc didn't go well?"

"Actually, they went marvelously. We're back together."

A wide smile split his face. "I knew it would only be a matter of
time. I'm happy for you, cousin."

"Thanks."

"So, what's going on? And don't tell me nothing. I just came
from your sisters, and both are acting weird."

Chevonne winced. "That's my fault. I shared some information
I learned today, and they're in shock."

"What kind of information?" he asked as he moved closer.

She looked around to see who was near before motioning him

even closer. For the next few moments, Chevonne filled him in on the Others. When she finished, Cillian didn't look surprised at all.

"I've heard of them," he told her. "You told me more than I knew, but the word on the street is mixed. Some tout them as the saviors of the Fae. Others are terrified. Lots of Fae have come up missing over the last few months. I'm beginning to think it's related to this group."

Chevonne smiled at someone who walked past. She then looked at Cillian. "I'm sure it's them. Stay away from anyone trying to recruit you."

"I've been asked to go to an event in a few days. I can't get an answer as to what it is."

"Don't chance it. Bow out," she urged. "Please."

Cillian smiled as he nodded. "I don't want any part of that. You don't have to worry."

"What of your brother? Your parents? Have you talked to them about it?"

At this, he rolled his eyes and took a drink of his adult beverage. "Our family isn't like yours. Before tonight, I hadn't seen my brother for months, and he wouldn't listen to anything I had to say anyway. As for my parents…well, do you really want me to go there?"

She bit back a laugh. It was a mystery to everyone why Lena and Colm O'Neill had gotten married. They rarely spent time together. Chevonne was happy that she was part of a family with such strong ties. Why her father and Cillian's mother were so different, no one knew.

"You should tell them anyway," she said.

Cillian nodded solemnly. "I think this is important enough to share. With everyone I know."

"I agree. Just be careful."

"Those Fae in all black you mentioned. I've seen them around the city a few times."

She touched Cillian's arm. "Don't engage. Give them a wide berth."

"You don't need to warn me. I'm a lover, not a fighter," he said with a wink.

Chevonne gave him a gentle shove. "You're impossible."

"It's why you love me."

"That I do." She leaned over and kissed him on the cheek.

After Cillian walked away, Chevonne continued around the room, stopping and talking to guests along the way. She was just about to let her parents know that she was leaving when her aunt took her by the arm and stopped her.

"Chevonne. As beautiful as ever," her aunt said with a smile.

Lena was an inch taller than Chevonne. She had always loved short hair and kept it in various hairstyles. Lena's gaze was direct and off-putting at times. "Hi, Aunt Lena."

"I've been waiting to speak to you. You're just like your mother and sisters, working the room the way you do."

Chevonne ignored the backhanded compliment and smiled. "It's what makes these parties such a success."

"I'm surprised you and your sisters still play such a part in them," Lena replied.

"Why wouldn't we?"

"I would've thought you'd have outgrown them."

Chevonne snorted. "Look around, Aunt Lena. There are only adults here. There's nothing to outgrow."

Lena smiled tightly. "Too true. I had thought you and Oscar might be making things official."

"We broke up. I'm back with Ruarc now."

"So I heard earlier."

Chevonne frowned. "Heard?"

"Your mother was quick to tell me about him coming back into your life. I hope you made him beg."

Chevonne might not like her aunt very much, but she had never wanted to get away from her as badly as she did at that moment. "I didn't."

"Odd that he came to you after all these centuries."

"I found him."

Lena's eyes widened in shock. "Really?"

"Yes. I love him."

"That's a perfect reason."

Chevonne tried to pull her arm free. "Excuse me, but I need to go see about something."

Her aunt's fingers dug into Chevonne's arm. "Not just yet, dear."

"Excuse me?" Chevonne asked, shocked at her aunt's tone and grip.

"You heard me."

Unease rippled through Chevonne. "Release me."

"When I'm done."

"With what?"

"Telling you what needs to be said," Lena snapped in a low voice, her silver eyes glittering dangerously.

Chevonne ground her teeth together as Lena's nails pierced her skin. She considered knocking her aunt back with a dose of magic, but she didn't want to cause a scene at her parents' party. Not until she figured out what was going on. Then, she would kick her aunt's arse.

"You were always such a good girl," Lena said. "Always doing what was expected. You shouldn't have a problem now."

Chevonne glanced down at her aunt's hand on her arm and quirked a brow. It was becoming harder and harder to keep her anger in check. "Spit it out. I have things to do."

"Like go back to Ruarc?"

"It's none of your business."

"Actually, it is. You made it my business when you pushed yourself into his flat."

Chevonne's blood turned to ice. "What are you talking about?"

"Come on. You're smarter than that."

Chevonne suddenly wished she had never left Ruarc's penthouse. Had she really believed that she would be safe at her parents' house? All the warnings Ruarc had given her rushed into her head. She fought the acrid taste of regret. She could call for Ruarc like she'd promised, but she knew that was the wrong thing to do.

She glanced around, hoping to find Cillian or someone to signal to come and help her. Chevonne gasped when Lena's nails sank deeper into her arm.

"Pay attention," her aunt snapped.

Chevonne jerked her gaze back to Lena and bit out, "What? What do you want from me?"

Her aunt chuckled, her smile back in place. "Perhaps I overestimated you. Have you not figured it out?"

"So, you're part of the Others. Somehow, that doesn't surprise me. You've always been a cold bitch."

Lena shot her a flat look. "Name-calling? Really? I thought you above such childish endeavors. I'm not just in the Others, niece. I lead the Six."

"You're lying." Chevonne wanted to run, hide, scream, something. *Anything*. But all she could do was stand and stare at her aunt in shock, her stomach sinking to her feet.

"Oh, I'm not." She pulled Chevonne close. "Behave yourself. I brought along some guests to ensure that you don't do anything stupid. Have a look."

Chevonne swallowed around the lump of fear in her throat and lifted her gaze. Her lips parted in dismay when she saw the Fae in black. With one glance, she counted six, and she hadn't even looked to the side or behind her.

"Exactly," Lena said. "You're going to listen very carefully, or I'm going to make a mess of things in here."

Chevonne glared at her aunt. She pressed her lips together in fear of letting Lena know exactly what she thought of her and the Others. The threat to her family was the only thing that kept her silent. Ruarc had warned her that the Others would use her if they could. He had told her to be careful. She had ignored him because she'd believed she was stronger, wiser, and smarter than other Fae. It had never occurred to her that someone close to her would not only be in the Others but *lead* them.

Just what had she gotten herself into?

More importantly, what did her aunt want?

Lena sighed dramatically. "I thought for sure Ruarc would have recognized me. Guess I didn't make that much of an impression at our little family soirees."

"What do you want?" Chevonne asked once more.

"The world."

Chevonne's entire body was cold now. She knew her aunt was serious, and that made Lena all the more dangerous.

"And you," Lena replied with a ruthless smile.

CHAPTER ELEVEN

The more time that passed without Chevonne's return, the more worried Ruarc became. Midnight came and went. He paced, glowered, brooded. Finally, he gave up and said her name. He kept telling himself that he was upset for nothing. That Chevonne had probably lost track of time. But he recognized the lie for what it was.

Ruarc thought about calling for Rordan. In the end, Ruarc decided to go to the party himself. The only reason Chevonne wouldn't have returned was if something had happened. There was no need to get the Reapers involved. This was Ruarc's problem. The Reapers wanted the Others gone, but would they halt in their planning to help him save the woman he loved? He didn't want to test that speculation. At least, not yet.

With a thought, he replaced his jeans and tee with a suit. He thought about Chevonne's parents' home and was just about to jump when she suddenly appeared in his living room. Ruarc rushed to her and wrapped his arms around her, holding her tighter than he should.

"I was getting worried."

She laughed softly. "I'm here. Everything is fine."

He pulled back and held her by the upper arms as he searched her face. "Are you all right? Did anything happen?"

"I'm just tired." She sighed softly. "I would've been here sooner, but it was difficult to get away."

Ruarc called his casual clothes back as Chevonne walked to the sideboard and poured herself a gin and tonic. Was it his imagination, or was something off? He and Chevonne hadn't been together in several centuries, but he hadn't noticed anything earlier. Then again, he hadn't been looking. It was probably all in his head. He'd gotten worried because he'd expected her back earlier, which then made him look for things that weren't there.

She sighed as she turned to him and took a drink. Then she walked to the sofa. As she sat, her mauve dress vanished, replaced by a beige cashmere lounge set. She curled her legs to the side to get comfortable.

"What?" she asked into the silence. "You know how exhausting those parties are."

He nodded, forcing himself to smile. "I do."

She patted the cushion beside her. "Sit. I'll fill you in on everything."

"All kinds of scenarios have been running through my head. It's a relief to see you back safely." He sank beside her and rested his arm on her legs. "I imagined soldiers showing up. Or Others making a scene."

Chevonne laughed and took another drink. "I did tell my family about the Others. Eileen had heard of them, though she knew very little. Shannon and my parents knew nothing. I managed to fill them in right before the first guests arrived."

"I hope your family was on high alert."

"The highest."

"Let's hope this keeps them safe."

She nodded. "I also told Cillian, who plans to share it with all of his acquaintances. It's good to get the word out."

"The more people who know the truth, the less likely they are to join."

"Exactly."

He studied her, unable to shake the feeling that something had happened at the party. "I wish I would've gone with you tonight."

"I told the family about us," she said with a smile.

"How did that go?"

She laughed softly and finished her drink. "No one seemed surprised in the least. Shannon told me she had been expecting such news for some time. We didn't talk about you long once I began telling them about the Others."

"Did you tell them I was mixed up in it?"

"I didn't. I think they all drew conclusions that I know about the Others because of you, but we didn't get too deep in the conversation because the party began. They're going to want to talk more."

He ran his hand up and down her leg, the cashmere soft beneath his palms. "Understandable."

"Did your friends return?"

"Not with any more news." Ruarc didn't know why he kept it from her that Rordan had, indeed, briefly returned and checked on her. He wasn't sure that Chevonne would be happy to learn that the Reaper had listened in on their conversations.

Or did he keep it from her for another reason?

Ruarc didn't want to dwell too long on those thoughts. He didn't like the direction they took him. If he kept things from Chevonne, it was because he didn't think he could trust her. After he had assured Rordan that they could.

Frustrated, Ruarc ran a hand through his hair. The threat of the Six had him doubting everyone, and that wasn't fair. Especially to Chevonne. She had no part in any of this. Of that, he was positive. Though, he couldn't shake the uneasy feeling that he'd gotten since she returned. It was probably just anxiety from waiting on her and thinking of all the horrible things that could have happened.

He glanced over to find Chevonne staring at him. For just an instant, he thought he saw shadows behind her eyes. He frowned as he shifted to face her. "Something on your mind?"

"I'm just sad that we can't have some peace and enjoy each other again."

"We will. Once the Others are taken care of."

She glanced down at her hands that held the tumbler. "You really think they can be defeated?"

"I do."

"You're going to fight, aren't you?"

He nodded slowly. "What kind of Fae would I be to sit back and let others do it?"

"The kind that would remain alive."

"Aye, but I wouldn't be me."

"You don't have the powers that the soldiers or your friends do. You've said so yourself."

Ruarc took one of her hands in his and rubbed his thumb along the back of it. "The Others and everything they stand for need to be halted before they do irrevocable harm."

"What if they already have?"

"Like anything that's rotting, you remove it and whatever decay is left. Then you start over."

Her smile was sad. "We could leave. Run away."

This wasn't the Chevonne he knew. She had never run from anything in her life. Granted, what she was dealing with now was much worse than anything before it, but it still caused him trepidation. "For all my family's faults, I can't leave them to be slaughtered by the soldiers and have their power given to the Six."

"Of course," she said, but she wouldn't hold his gaze.

That's when Ruarc realized that this might be too much for her. This wasn't just Dark fighting Light. This was a group of Fae with untapped power, who took whatever they wanted. "Maybe you and your family should go somewhere until things are resolved."

He half expected her to snap her gaze up to his and tell him that she wasn't going anywhere. Instead, she toyed with the hem of her shirt. It was wrong for Ruarc to be hurt by her silence, but he couldn't help how he felt. Not after all the things she had declared and promised earlier that day. Once more, he suspected that something had happened at the party that she didn't want to tell him.

"Where would we go?" she finally asked, shrugging slightly. She glanced up at him. "Besides, I doubt I could convince my family to leave Dublin."

"You would have to leave more than the city. The Others are spread throughout Ireland."

She snorted. "We won't go anywhere."

"Try. You said they wanted to talk more. Maybe you can convince them to leave."

Chevonne shrugged again. "I will."

The more he spoke with her, the more he felt like she was putting up a wall. Almost as if she didn't want him to get close.

Or she could be exhausted from what she had discovered that day, telling her family, and then the party. She had put on a brave face earlier, but Ruarc knew she was frightened. That in and of itself took a toll on someone—mentally, physically, and emotionally.

"Why don't we go to bed? You look worn out," he said.

Chevonne stood. "That's a good idea. If you still want me here."

"Of course, I do." He reached for her hand as he got to his feet.

She set her tumbler on the island as they walked past and headed to the bedroom. Ruarc hoped that whatever was causing his anxiety about Chevonne would be gone when he woke.

Isle of Skye

Balladyn stood on the windswept mountain and looked out over the sea. The fifty-mile-long island was the largest of the Inner Hebrides and had stunning scenery and breathtaking landscapes. With its medieval castles, charming fishing villages, and rugged countryside, it was a destination that called to all, be they Dragon Kings, Fae, Druids, or mortals. The isle wasn't just beautiful, it was magical.

Hence why it drew so many.

Balladyn had wanted to hate the isle from the very beginning.

How could he love anything that was Scottish and therefore part of the Dragon Kings? But the isle had taken a piece of his soul and held it firmly, refusing to let go.

Skye had played an integral part for the Fae. The Warriors and Druids from MacLeod Castle had learned of the Fae at the Fairy Pools. At one time, the Fairy Pools had been important to the Druids and mortals. That wasn't the case anymore. So much had changed in the last handful of years thanks to the original Others.

"You're quiet," Cathal said from beside him.

Balladyn looked at his friend and shrugged. "Thinking."

"Shhh," Sorcha, Cathal's mate, who was a Halfing as well as a Druid said. "Let me enjoy this for just a moment."

Balladyn slid his gaze to the valley below where Sorcha's cousin's cottage sat. He had his doubts about involving Rhona, the leader of the Skye Druids—or any of the Druids—in their plans to guard Ruarc's family, mainly because the Druids were putting together their own group of Others.

The entire thing made Balladyn want to roll his eyes. No one looked at history anymore. No one paid attention to the past and the actions of others and made decisions. Instead, they focused on the current scenarios to plot and scheme for power. It was all about dominance.

He should know. For a brief time, he had been King of the Dark.

"I'm ready," Sorcha finally said.

Balladyn and Cathal, who held Sorcha's hand, remained veiled as they teleported to the cottage. When Cathal nodded, Balladyn walked around the cottage to look for patrols of any kind. He returned and shook his head, indicating that the coast was clear. Only then did he and Cathal lower their veils. Sorcha then released Cathal's hand and walked to the door to knock.

A moment later, the door opened to reveal a tall, lithe redhead in a green shirt and jeans. Her gaze moved from Sorcha to Cathal and finally Balladyn. The light above the door showed her classic beauty and large, green eyes.

Rhona quirked a brow. "I take it this isn't a social visit."

"I wish it was," Sorcha said.

Cathal nodded at Rhona. "We've come to ask for your help with a particular situation."

"Guarding a Fae family against the Fae Others," Sorcha added.

Rhona's gaze slid briefly to Balladyn as the silence stretched. Finally, the Druid leader stepped aside. "You three had better come inside then."

CHAPTER TWELVE

Chevonne stared at the wall as she lay on her side, Ruarc's arm draped over her. He wasn't asleep either. The minutes had ticked by slowly as they lay in silence. Her mind filled with thoughts of her encounter with her aunt. Disgust, loathing, and horror churned violently within her.

Not that long ago, she had assured Ruarc that he would get out of the predicament the Six had put him in. She'd believed that she understood the position in which he found himself. With the Reapers helping, she was sure that he would triumph. All of that had changed at the party when her aunt confronted her.

A way out? She only wished there was such a thing for her. She now truly comprehended Ruarc's angst and panic. Because they were her constant companions now.

She wanted to tell him everything. It killed her to keep things from him. An impossible situation. They were both in one. The difference was, he could turn to the Reapers. She had no one.

"Don't test me. You know what I'm capable of."

Her aunt's words from the party echoed in Chevonne's head.

The worst part of the night hadn't been learning that Lena led the Six. It was not rushing to her family to alert them.

Chevonne had watched her sisters and parents mingle with guests, laughing and talking without a care in the world. They had no idea of the evil inside their walls—or the threat that hung over them.

Chevonne's stomach roiled when she recalled her conversation with her aunt.

Lena gleefully smiled. "Ruarc was just a pawn. We took him because of his connection to the Reapers and to you, my dear. I offered Oscar a spot in the organization if he could get you to a meeting."

"Why?" Chevonne demanded.

"Where you go, Cillian will follow. Once both of you are a part of things, your sisters and parents will join."

Chevonne swallowed the bile that rose in her throat. "What of your son?"

"He's exactly where he should be. Exactly where you'll be soon."

"And if I refuse?"

Lena laughed dryly. "You won't. In case you need an incentive, I'll kill your family and Cillian. It won't be quick. It will be painful and slow. And you'll watch every second of it."

Ruarc had warned her that this would happen. Chevonne alternated between wanting to vomit and the desire to hit something. This couldn't be happening to her. But she would endure all of this and then return to Ruarc, where she would tell him everything. Between the two of them, they would figure out what to do.

"Before you think of telling Ruarc about our little chat, you should know that—"

"That you'll kill me," Chevonne said over her.

Lena lifted a brow and stared at her for a long moment. "Don't interrupt me again."

It killed Chevonne to sit there and listen and not start screaming her head off. She caught sight of the soldiers out of the corner of her eye and wanted to cry in outrage.

"Now, as I was saying," Lena continued. "As long as you don't share any of this with Ruarc, I'll spare his life. No matter the outcome, he will live."

It was more than Chevonne expected to hear. The knowledge of a guarantee that Ruarc wouldn't die was enough for her to seriously consider things. So her aunt wanted her to join the Others. That didn't mean she had to actually go through with it or participate. And being inside the organization might be exactly what was needed to bring them down. That, coupled with Ruarc's life, made her decision.

"Fine," Chevonne bit out. "I'll join."

"Oh, it won't be that easy," her aunt said with a wicked smile. "You have one more important thing to do."

"What more could you possibly want from me?"

The smile her aunt gave Chevonne sent chills through her. "The Reapers."

Chevonne squeezed her eyes closed as a tear fell from a corner and dropped onto the bed. She didn't want to betray Ruarc or the Reapers, but if she didn't, her family would die horrible deaths. Just as Ruarc was part of the Others to keep his family alive, she would do what she had to do for hers.

Hopefully, she could live with herself after.

Ruarc might never forgive her, though. But he would understand her predicament since it was similar to his. Not to mention, he would be alive. That was something.

She wiped at her tear as another followed. If she started crying now, she wouldn't be able to stop. Ruarc would know that something was wrong and pressure her to tell him. She wanted nothing more than to share her worry with someone, but Ruarc's very life depended on her keeping everything secret.

Ruarc feared the Six. The Reapers took the Six seriously.

How could she do anything else?

She had never cared for Lena. Her aunt had always been cool and reserved to everyone, even her brother, Hugo. Chevonne's father used to tell her that Lena had always been that way. It didn't matter who she was with, or what she did, she was detached from everyone and everything. Not even marriage and motherhood had changed that. Chevonne didn't care what the reasoning was. She hated her aunt now. It took a vile nature for someone to do the things that Lena did.

Sunlight began filling the room, signaling a new day. She wasn't ready to face it—or Ruarc. He was keenly perceptive. He'd always been able to see through anything she tried. She would have to come up with some lie to keep this from him.

Then there were the Reapers. Ruarc thought highly of them—

or at least Rordan. Chevonne only knew what little Ruarc had told her. They seemed capable enough with a goddess and god on their side. Why wouldn't they just take out the Others? It would save her and Ruarc—and probably countless others.

And that was the rub. The Reapers hadn't obliterated the Others because they couldn't. Now, she and her family—and Ruarc and his—were in the crosshairs.

She could tell the Reapers. Lena hadn't stated that in their agreement, but that was splitting hairs. Knowing her aunt, that might be the very thing that would cost Ruarc, his family, and hers their lives. Could she take the chance? Should she?

Ruarc kissed her shoulder as he snuggled closer to her. "Morning."

She wasn't ready for this, but ready or not, the day had dawned. Her only bet was to make an excuse to leave for a while. She had laid the groundwork by saying that her family wanted to talk more about the Others. That would give her some breathing room, but she couldn't stay away for too long. Lena wanted information on the Reapers. Chevonne still didn't understand how she had known that Ruarc and the Reapers were working together.

Ruarc rolled her onto her back as he propped himself up on an elbow and searched her face with his pale silver gaze. The black rings around his irises seemed wider this morning. "Did you sleep well?"

"I did," she lied with a smile.

He gave her a crooked grin. "I'm happy to wake up next to you again. I never thought it would be possible."

"I love you," she suddenly said and fought a wave of tears.

His brows snapped together as he gently touched her face. "I love you. You would tell me if something was wrong, wouldn't you?"

"You know I would. I'm just so happy to have you back in my life." That wasn't a lie. It wasn't the whole truth, but it wasn't a lie.

"You can tell me anything. You know that, right?"

She forced a smile that she didn't feel. "I do."

"Von, I know something happened last night. Please tell me

what it is. Were your parents upset about us? Your sisters? They said something negative, didn't they?"

She parted her lips, trying to find something to say when someone cleared their throat from the kitchen.

"Bloody hell," Ruarc murmured as he turned and rolled out of bed. In two steps, he'd dressed in jeans and a maroon sweater.

Chevonne covered her face with her hands when she was alone. Then she threw off the comforter and called a pair of dark denim jeans to her, along with a slate-colored sweater and brown boots. She shook out her hair and pulled it back into a low ponytail. A quick look at her reflection in the bathroom mirror satisfied her.

She drew in a deep breath before leaving the room. When she walked out, she saw Rordan with Ruarc, standing at the dining table and looking at a map. Chevonne glanced around to see if anyone else was in the flat. Ruarc had said that the Reapers could remain veiled for longer than any other Fae. One could be there now, and she'd never know it.

A part of her wished one had witnessed everything with Lena at the party. That way, she wouldn't have to keep such a secret.

When the conversation stopped, Chevonne looked up to find both men watching her. Ruarc had a frown on his face as he stood with Rordan at the table where a three-dimensional map of Dublin sat. Ruarc had given her an out by thinking that her family must have said something about him. She didn't want to lie, but if she didn't...

"I didn't mean to interrupt," she told them.

Ruarc shook his head. "You didn't. The plan is in place. We're doing it today."

Her stomach fell like lead to her feet. "Today?" In one aspect, she wouldn't have to carry on with the lie for very much longer. On the other, Ruarc would learn the truth about her hand in the Reapers' capture.

Rordan's silver eyes were penetrating as he watched her. "You're pale."

"I'm not a morning person," she quipped and plastered a smile on her face.

That seemed to pacify Ruarc, but Rordan continued scrutinizing her for a few more moments. She walked on wooden legs to the kitchen and procured coffee with her magic. She didn't dare drink it, though. One taste and it would all come up.

"You know what to do," Rordan said as the map disappeared from the table.

Ruarc nodded, smiling. "I do."

"Don't worry about your family, either. They're being guarded."

"By Reapers?" Ruarc asked.

Rordan shook his head. "They'll be safe."

"What if things go badly?" Chevonne asked.

The minute the words were out, she wanted to take them back. Both men turned to her. She felt exposed under their scrutiny. She swallowed, the sound loud to her ears.

"It won't," Ruarc said.

Rordan's gaze narrowed slightly. "Do you worry we won't succeed?"

"I'm just…ah…thinking of all possibilities. It's good to be prepared."

Ruarc crossed his arms over his chest. "Hopefully, whoever is watching my family will be able to take on the soldiers if we lose. By then, the Six will know I've turned against them and will seek to fulfill their promise."

Rordan said nothing more. He looked at Ruarc and nodded before vanishing.

"Will the Six be there?" she asked.

Ruarc twisted his lips. "I doubt it. They'll most likely send soldiers."

"I thought the Six wanted to end the Reapers and Death."

"They do, but they seclude themselves so no one can get to them."

She almost told him that wasn't entirely true. "This isn't our war. We shouldn't be fighting it."

He cocked his head to the side as he frowned. "How do you not believe this is our war? This involves the Fae. Thousands have already died. We could be next. Isn't that worth fighting for?"

"Yes. Of course, it is. I don't know what I was thinking."

"You're scared, as anyone would be." He walked to her and rested his hands on her hips. "The Reapers have been standing against the Others. It shouldn't rest only with them."

She smoothed her hands over his sweater as she stared at his chest. "If the Others hadn't kidnapped and forced you, would you stand against them?"

"Yes. The difference is, I know war. You've never been in battle. You have every right to be scared and worried. If you want to run and take your family, do it. Now."

She rested her head on his chest and closed her eyes when his arms came around her. "I told you, I'm not leaving you."

"It might be safer if you did."

"We don't know how far their reach stretches. I'd rather be here where I know what's happening."

He kissed the top of her head.

"Is it really happening today?"

"Yes," he replied softly.

She squeezed her eyes closed. "Where?"

"A warehouse in Rosemont Business Park."

Her heart thudded painfully. "How is it going to happen?"

"I'm going to alert the Others that I'm meeting with my friends. The Others will think they're setting a trap, but it's actually a trap for them."

"Won't the Six train more soldiers once those are dead?"

"Who says the Reapers are going to kill them?"

She pulled back to look at him. "What if the Six come?"

"Even better. It's them the Reapers are really after. The last time they met, the Six lost one. I think the Six are afraid to meet Death and the Reapers one-on-one."

Chevonne smiled. "Sounds like it. Is it an equal match between the Six and the Reapers?"

"Not even close. There are more Reapers."

"That's good. How many are there?"

"Ten," Ruarc replied.

Chevonne filed that information away. "How much time do we have?"

"None. I need to go now. The sooner I tell the Others about this, the sooner all of this can end, and I can have my life back. Our life," he corrected with a smile as he lowered his head to kiss her. "I'll return as soon as possible."

Before she could stop him, he was gone.

Chevonne fisted her hands and curled into herself as she opened her mouth on a silent scream and gave in to the tears. She angrily wiped away any evidence of her crying and took a few calming breaths. Then she walked out of the flat to the hallway and called for her aunt.

Lena was there a heartbeat later. "Well?"

"Ruarc is contacting you now. They're setting a trap for you in a warehouse in the Rosemont Business area."

Her aunt smiled. "That wasn't so hard, was it?"

"Fek off."

"Such language. Your father should've slapped your face a time or two to curb that defiant streak of yours."

Chevonne took a step back. "I did my part. I told you about the Reapers and didn't tell Ruarc anything. I'm done."

"You're just getting started," Lena said and reached for her.

CHAPTER THIRTEEN

It was easy to find the soldiers. Too easy, in fact. Ruarc had known they were watching him. The moment he appeared outside his building, two of the bastards stepped out of the shadows. There were more, but he didn't care. Once he told them where he was meeting the Reapers, he turned and walked away.

Ruarc was glad to have that part finished. He was one step closer to being free of the Others so he could return to his life with Chevonne. His smile slipped as he thought of her. He'd known that something was wrong. He should've guessed that her family would cause a scene about them getting back together.

Granted, his family wasn't as prominent as hers, but they weren't the worst, either. Though, to be fair, if he had a daughter, he wouldn't want her anywhere near someone with his family's history. He could understand their thinking. That didn't mean he had to like it. But he'd prove to them how much he loved Chevonne.

Ruarc didn't immediately go back to his penthouse because he suspected that Chevonne needed some time to herself. And he wanted to think. So much hinged on the plans turning out perfectly this afternoon. He didn't doubt the Reapers and their abilities. He'd

seen them fight at the Others' compound. He understood why the
Others were adamant about their removal.

Maybe Ruarc would get to meet Death. He'd seen her at the
battle, as well. She had been fierce. All of them had.

He'd also like to meet the rest of the Reapers. He knew he'd
only seen a portion of them. He had no idea how many there were.
He shouldn't have lied to Chevonne, but he wasn't sure of the
Reapers' exact number.

Ruarc wished he had the abilities the Reapers had. It would
make fighting the Others easier. No doubt, Rordan would try to
keep him out of the battle, but that wasn't going to happen. He had
skills. They might not be a match for the faster and more powerful
soldiers, but that didn't lessen his need to be a part of the fight.

He walked around for another twenty minutes before teleporting
to his penthouse. He wanted to spend as much time with Chevonne
as he could before the battle. Except, she wasn't in the flat.

"Von," he called, his concern mounting.

He waited for her to appear. With each minute that passed in
silence, a knot of panic formed. Then he remembered that her
family had wanted to have a longer conversation about the Others.
Still, he wished she would've left him a note or sent a text,
something so he wouldn't worry.

Ruarc stood at the living room window and looked out over the
city. Humans milled about like ants hurrying to and fro, absorbed in
their lives, completely unaware that other beings were on their
realm—and that an important battle was about to take place.

His shoulders lifted as he took a deep breath and then slowly
released it. Once more, the certainty that he wouldn't live to see the
night reared its ugly head. He wasn't afraid of dying, but he'd finally
found happiness again. And he wasn't ready to let it go. He could
leave the battle once it began.

Ruarc snorted. He wouldn't leave. He'd never be able to look at
himself in a mirror again if he did. Which meant, he would remain
—even if it cost him his life. He pivoted and looked around his flat.
He missed seeing Chevonne walking among his things. She was the
only one for him. He'd known that from the first time he saw her.

The life they could have together would be beautiful and amazing. He pictured them with children, laughing and happy. There would be ups and downs, as all relationships had, but their love would get them through anything that came their way.

It was a dream he'd had when they were first together. When he walked away from her, it had faded, seeming forever out of reach. But she had returned, and with her, the certainty of their future. Fate wouldn't be so malicious as to dangle such a perfect future before him again, only to yank it away at the last second.

Ruarc walked to the sofa and sat. He created an orb that filled his hand. This one wasn't for defense. The iridescent colors swirled in a stunning, chaotic fashion. Mirrored back at him was his face. He smiled as the orb began to record him.

"Hello, beautiful," he began.

Ruarc finished the recording and rose to put the orb on the nightstand next to the bed. He found Rordan and another Reaper with long, black and silver hair and red eyes waiting for him when he walked from his room.

"This is Balladyn," Rordan said.

Ruarc raised a brow. "The former King of the Dark?"

"And leader of the Queen's Guard," Rordan added.

Ruarc was shocked to be standing before such a legendary Fae. Revered by the Light before becoming Dark and taking the throne.

Balladyn bowed his head. "You're doing a very brave thing."

"It's the right thing to do," Ruarc replied.

Rordan grinned at Balladyn. "Now do you see why we got along so well?"

Balladyn chuckled, his lips pulling into a smile. "I do."

"Is it time?" Ruarc asked.

Rordan returned his attention to him. "We've had Reapers set up at the warehouse since last night. Soldiers began arriving a short time ago."

"Just as planned," Ruarc said with a nod. "They think they'll arrive before any of you."

Balladyn crossed his arms over his chest. "They keep doing the reveal spell to see if any of us are there and veiled."

"But we're quicker," Rordan replied with a grin.

Ruarc looked over his shoulder toward the bedroom. "I'd hoped to see Chevonne before I left."

"Where did she go?" Balladyn asked.

Ruarc didn't want to tell them the truth, but it was better they knew, just in case. "I'm not sure. I think to her parents'. She told them about the Others last night to warn them against getting recruited. She told me they wanted to discuss things further."

"Have you called for her?" Rordan asked.

Once more, Ruarc hesitated. His answer made Chevonne look bad, but he had no choice. "I have. She's not returned."

"That doesn't bode well," Balladyn replied.

Rordan slowly shook his head. "No, it does not."

"Chevonne would never join the Others. Not after what I told her." Ruarc didn't like the way the two Reapers looked at him. Anger burned hotly through him. "She would never betray me."

Balladyn lowered his arms to his side. "Maybe not willingly."

"No. She would've told me. She knows how important all of this is," Ruarc argued.

Rordan smiled, but it didn't reach his eyes. "Let's hope you're right."

He had to be. But the uneasiness that had been swirling in his gut since his return made him doubt. He hated the suspicion, loathed the distrust that her absence created.

Then he had a thought. "Could the Others have taken her to ensure that I comply with their demands?"

"It's possible," Rordan replied.

But the skepticism in the Reapers' eyes said otherwise.

Ruarc ran his hands down his face and blew out a breath. Then he looked between the two men. "The Others have made it so no one feels they can trust anyone else. I'm putting my family's lives in your hands. I don't do that lightly. I do it because I have faith that the Reapers can triumph and end the Others."

"We believe you," Balladyn said.

Rordan lifted one shoulder in a shrug. "We wouldn't be here otherwise."

"Understood."

Balladyn caught his gaze. "Once the fighting starts, we don't expect you to stay."

"I'm not leaving," Ruarc declared.

Rordan's black brows snapped together. "Remaining would be suicide."

"I know battle. I may not have the strength and power of Reapers or the soldiers, but I'm not going to sit on the sidelines and watch. The Six dragged me into this. I want everyone to know which side I chose."

Balladyn and Rordan exchanged a smile. Then Rordan said, "I told the Reapers you'd say that."

"No one will think less of you if you leave," Balladyn added.

Ruarc nodded in acknowledgement. "Should we get this party started?"

"We'll teleport after you to the warehouse. We'll be veiled, so you won't see or hear us," Rordan advised.

Ruarc took one more look at his flat. He'd wanted to wrap his arms around Chevonne and give her a lingering kiss before leaving. He prayed that she was safe. He hoped that she was simply embroiled in a deep discussion with her family that prevented her from responding to him. He thought of the mobile and briefly asked Rordan to wait as he placed a call, but there wasn't time for that now.

He was tired of having the Others watching him. Threatening him. They had made him feel as if he had nowhere to turn. He should've remembered that Rordan was a man of honor. He should've sought his help as soon as everything went sideways. Fear and mistrust had kept Ruarc silent. But he woudln't be quiet anymore.

"Let's go," he said, right before jumping to the warehouse.

Ruarc appeared in the parking lot in front of the warehouse with dark blue siding. To anyone watching, he looked as if he were alone. He trusted that Rordan and Balladyn were with him as promised. The Reapers hadn't threatened him. They hadn't endangered his family. They had offered him a way out.

Were the Reapers powerful? Yes. Were they formidable? Absolutely. But they had been working behind the scenes for untold eons. Not once had they tried to take control of the Fae or any race of beings. They hadn't exuded their power over others simply because they could. That was the difference between the Reapers and the Others.

Smooth words could sway anyone—even the Fae. He was shocked and saddened that the Others had misled so many of his fellow Fae. Their hold had to be broken. If the Dragon Kings could triumph over the original Others, who had centuries to plan out their attacks, then the Fae could defeat this enemy. They had no choice. Either they did it…or the Dragon Kings would interfere and drive the Fae from Earth once and for all.

Where would that leave the Fae? They had no other home, not since their power struggle destroyed the Fae Realm. Now, they were about to lose another home because of the same thing. They hadn't learned the first time. Maybe they would this time.

Ruarc squared his shoulders and started toward the warehouse door. It was small compared to the rest of the building. He used magic to open it before he reached it. Ruarc cautiously stepped inside. It was a new warehouse. Utterly empty of even debris or dirt. The concrete floor was thick, the ceilings soared overhead, and the many windows on his level and higher up shed light within. Dust particles twirled in the sunlight that streamed in from the outside.

His boots made a muffled sound as he walked to the center of the warehouse. The cool January air had an electric feel, one Ruarc hadn't experienced since his days in the army. He'd been a good soldier. He'd wanted to make a career out of it, and his superiors had welcomed that ambition. It might have been a while since he'd been in combat, but it wasn't something he would ever forget. That training was muscle memory. His palm itched for a weapon as his magic surged through him, waiting to be called.

Ruarc halted in the middle of the warehouse. This was a safe place to have a skirmish without any mortals seeing. He had no doubt that soldiers would lose their lives to the Reapers today. Could

Reapers die? Ruarc hoped to hell they couldn't because there were fewer of them than the soldiers.

He looked left, then right. If the Six arrived, all of this could end today. If, if, *if*. He didn't let his thoughts linger on his family or even Chevonne. He needed to immerse himself in everything around him because he had no doubt that the instant the Others realized he had betrayed them, they would come after him.

Rordan appeared in front of him. Their gazes met.

The show was about to begin.

CHAPTER FOURTEEN

Something about the beginning of a battle always made Ruarc feel calm. All nervousness and anxiousness evaporated. Leaving him composed and relaxed.

Movement on his other side caught his attention. Ruarc looked to find five soldiers. He swiveled his head and found that four Reapers had joined Rordan. Tension crackled through the air as the two groups stared at each other. Ruarc knew more Reapers were around, just as he knew there were more soldiers. He stood between the two units, each glaring at the other.

"What the fek?" Rordan demanded of Ruarc in a fake tone of irritation.

Ruarc owed Rordan, the Reapers, and Death a great deal when all this was over. In response, Ruarc shook his head. "I don't know."

Their little show had better work to save his family. He was counting on it doing just that.

"What are you wankers waiting for?" one of the Reapers asked the soldiers.

The soldier nearest Ruarc asked, "The other five of you can show yourselves now. It'll make things easier for you."

Ruarc jerked as if punched. Where had the soldier gotten that number? He turned his head to Rordan in time to see a small frown cross the Reaper's features.

"You think there's only ten of us?" Balladyn asked with a grin.

Rordan's gaze met his, and he saw the sorrow in his friend's eyes. Ruarc's stomach roiled as comprehension dawned. He had told Chevonne there were ten Reapers. He knew there were at least that many. The only way the Others could know the number ten was from Chevonne. Which meant...she had betrayed him.

And the Reapers knew.

Rage against the Others consumed him as Ruarc turned to the soldiers and called his sword to him, just as an orb of magic formed in his left hand. Rordan moved to his right as Balladyn came up on his left.

Ruarc didn't know who threw the first strike. One moment, they were standing and glaring at each other. And the next, orbs were flying. Ruarc used his sword to slice the balls of magic coming too close to him. He spun, dodged, dove, and slid out of the way, all the while throwing his own orbs.

The soldiers moved blindingly fast, as did the Reapers. Ruarc began to think he might get out of this alive until a ball landed on his right shoulder. He gritted his teeth as searing agony took him, but he somehow managed to move out of the way as another orb came at him.

Suddenly, a soldier was in front of him. Ruarc tossed his sword to his left hand and used the blade to block the fighter's downward strike. The Fae screamed as Ruarc's sword severed his arm. Ruarc used the opportunity to shove an orb of magic into the soldier's face with his right hand.

The pain of using his injured arm was immense, but Ruarc couldn't give in to it. If he did, he would be dead. So, he clenched his teeth and concentrated on continuing to dodge the never-ending balls of magic. Ruarc managed to hold his own. Right up until he tripped and went down on one knee so hard, he heard the bone crack.

A soldier moved in front of Ruarc, a smile of glee on his face as he prepared to throw two orbs at him. He never got the chance as a black blade swung over Ruarc and severed the soldier's head from his body.

Ruarc climbed to his feet and found himself staring down at a petite woman dressed in battle armor. Her lavender eyes briefly met his before she turned to continue fighting. Death had just saved his life. Ruarc turned back to the fight. He had no idea how many Reapers or soldiers there were. For every soldier that fell, three more took their place.

He gripped his sword tighter in his left hand. His right shoulder was healing, but too slowly for battle. It would prohibit his movements. He held his arm protectively against his side and kept an orb of magic waiting in his uplifted palm, just in case.

Somehow, Ruarc remained on his feet. His injured knee and shoulder reminded him to keep moving. He killed another soldier before he saw something bright out of the corner of his eye. When he looked, he spotted Chevonne standing with the leader of the Six. And that's when he recognized the woman.

Lena, Chevonne's aunt.

Chevonne had tried to attack her aunt the moment they arrived at the warehouse, but Lena was too quick for her. She grabbed Chevonne's hands and bound them with magic behind her back.

"Stupid girl," Lena bit out.

The last place Chevonne wanted to be was at the warehouse. She didn't want to witness the battle. But, more importantly, she didn't want Ruarc to see her. Unfortunately, that was exactly what her aunt wanted.

Chevonne stared in disbelief as five Reapers stood against five soldiers with Ruarc in the middle. Her heart clutched painfully. She wanted to call out to him. To warn him to leave. But one word from her would seal her family's fate as well as Ruarc's.

Then the soldier mentioned ten Reapers. Chevonne didn't think anything of it until she saw a look pass between the Reapers, then saw the exchange between Rordan and Ruarc. Her lips parted in horror as a look of rage crossed over Ruarc's face. He had told her that there were ten Reapers, and she had passed that information on to her aunt. Now, Ruarc knew that she was the one who had betrayed him.

"I fekking hate you," Chevonne said to her aunt.

Lena chuckled at her outburst. "You'll thank me years from now."

"Never."

Her aunt didn't reply since her attention was on the battle. Chevonne didn't want to look, but she couldn't tear her eyes away from Ruarc. He wasn't nearly as quick as the others, but he held his ground, blocking and dodging the magic aimed at him, proving once more that he was highly skilled in the art of battle.

She cringed when his shoulder got injured. Chevonne silently urged him back to the battle, and nearly jumped with joy when he killed a soldier. She glanced around, trying to see who might be a threat to Ruarc, when he suddenly tripped and dropped to one knee. She managed to cut off the scream that formed. Then her gaze locked on a female warrior who saved Ruarc with a black sword.

Her aunt made a sound that drew her attention. Chevonne looked at Lena to see her face contorted with hatred as she glared at the woman fighting with the Reapers. That must be the goddess Death.

Chevonne's body tensed every time Ruarc engaged with a soldier. He was injured and without the extra powers the Reapers and soldiers had, and yet, he didn't back down.

"He would've made a great addition to my battalion," Lena said. "He could've led them. Too bad he's going to die today."

"We had a deal," Chevonne said in disbelief. But she should've seen this coming.

Lena laughed. "Did you honestly think I would hold to that? Aww. That's sweet and incredibly naïve."

Chevonne spat on her aunt.

Lena stilled before slowly lifting her hand and wiping away the gob. Fury blazed in her gaze when she looked at Chevonne. "Don't think I won't hurt you simply because you're family."

"You don't understand the meaning of that word."

"I understand it better than you."

When Chevonne looked away, her gaze clashed with Ruarc's. The hurt and disbelief she saw on his face was like a dagger to her heart. Before she could blink, he turned his back on her. And she knew that the action had been symbolic. Maybe she would get a chance to tell him why she had done what she had. She would find a way. Because he needed to know that she wasn't against him. She'd had no choice.

"I think he's a little angry with you," Lena said with a chuckle.

Chevonne had never hated anyone as much as she did her aunt at the moment. "You won't win. Nothing you're trying to do will succeed."

"We have more of a foothold than you think. We won't just succeed; we'll rule this planet."

Chevonne turned her head to Lena. "What of the Dragon Kings? Do you honestly think they'll allow that to happen?"

"By the time they figure out what's going on, they won't have a choice but to bow to us."

"Do you forget that one of the most powerful Fae to walk this realm is married to the King of Dragon Kings?"

Lena rolled her eyes. "Rhi is too busy with her role as Con's mate. She doesn't even know the Fae council she has worked so hard to set in motion is crumbling away."

Chevonne looked back to the battle. Her heart jumped into her throat when she didn't find Ruarc at first. When she finally located him, she almost cried when she saw how battered he was, how injured, and yet he was still on his feet.

She wanted to scream in frustration when another dozen soldiers arrived. But suddenly there were more Reapers, and they moved through the Others quickly and effectively. Almost as if they had been waiting for just that moment. Her chest hurt to know that the Reapers knew of her duplicity and had set things in motion because of it. They hadn't told Ruarc beforehand, however. She wasn't sure if that was the kinder option or not.

The tide of the battle was turning in the Reapers' favor. They weren't unscathed—most of them had various wounds on their bodies. Death and another Fae were even quicker than the Reapers and soldiers and did the most damage.

Chevonne didn't hide her smile. She might have been forced to do her aunt's bidding, but she was cheering the Reapers on. That smile died when her aunt suddenly appeared in front of Ruarc.

They were going to win this battle. Ruarc could see it through the blood and sweat in his eyes. But he didn't relent. More soldiers could appear like last time. He plunged his blade into an enemy's chest. When the soldier hurled an orb at his face, Ruarc leaned back and watched the ball sail over him toward Rordan.

Ruarc called out his name. Rordan turned in time to deflect the orb into another soldier. Ruarc straightened and twisted his sword before yanking it out and slicing off the soldier's head. The instant the soldier dropped; Lena stood before him.

"Chevonne sends her regards," Lena said, right before she propelled two orbs into his chest.

The pain was instant, sinking through his clothes and into his skin and muscle, then deeper into his bones. He stared into Lena's silver eyes and watched as they turned red, signaling that he was her first murder.

Dimly, he heard someone screaming. His eyes grew unfocused as he began falling backward. He tried to hold onto his sword, but it slipped from his fingers to clatter to the concrete. He was dying. Just as he'd known he would.

There was much he hadn't said. Much he hadn't done. But it didn't matter now.

The world went black. He couldn't fight it. He didn't want to fight it.

"Noooooooooooooooooooooooooooo!" Chevonne screamed when she saw Lena kill Ruarc.

She tried to run to him, but strong arms held her still. She struggled against them as the tears fell onto her cheeks.

The sight of Ruarc turning to ash took all the fight out of Chevonne.

CHAPTER FIFTEEN

The image of Ruarc's handsome face turning gray before disintegrating to ash played in Chevonne's head like a movie, over and over again. There had been shouting, and rough hands had grabbed her, but she hadn't been able to do anything. She was too shocked and numb to do anything.

The slap across her face jolted her. Her head whipped to the side as pain radiated across her cheekbone to her head and down her neck. Fury took hold and simmered dangerously. The need to lash out and hurt those who had dared to take Ruarc from her was strong. But if she wanted to prevail, she needed to be smart.

Chevonne slowly turned her head and faced her aunt. Lena quirked a brow as if she were surprised that Chevonne hadn't retaliated. If only her aunt knew the things she wanted to do to her —she wouldn't stand there so confidently.

"Did you honestly think I would let him live?" Lena demanded.

Chevonne seethed with righteous anger. "You will pay for what you've done."

"Who would dare to try? You?" Lena laughed. "You think because your parents had you and your sisters trained, that you can stand against me? I thought you were more intelligent than that."

For the first time, Chevonne looked around. She realized too late that she had been taken from the warehouse. She had no idea where she was, but she would find a way to get out. Just as she would find a way to have her revenge. The spacious room had large windows. A white desk sat in the corner with a white office chair. Two other white chairs sat before the desk. A beautiful ornate fireplace in white marble was situated on the opposite wall. A lush sofa in golden velvet with two matching chairs and a glass coffee table between them rested in the middle of the room.

Lena turned away and walked to her desk. "I have a list of things you'll do for me."

Chevonne saw her aunt bend to grab the paper. A quick look behind her said they were alone. Chevonne teleported to her parents' house. "Mum! Da!" she called as she raced through the house.

But there was no answer.

Her heart thudded against her ribs. She searched every room before she jumped to Eileen's house. When she couldn't find her, Chevonne teleported to Shannon's. Fear rippled through her. Lena had promised to leave her family alone if she did what her aunt wanted.

"She said she wouldn't kill them," Chevonne said aloud as comprehension dawned. "Mum. Da. Eileen. Shannon," she called, hoping one of them would appear.

Seconds ticked by with nothing. She didn't have time to wait. Anxiety took hold because Lena wouldn't have let her teleport without a reason.

Chevonne went to The Stag's Head for Cillian. She didn't want to tell her cousin who his mother was, but she didn't have a choice.

"Where's Cillian?" she asked a server that she nearly collided with.

The tall blonde shrugged. "Haven't seen him since yesterday."

Next, Chevonne went to Cillian's flat. But he wasn't there, either. A sob lodged in her throat. Everyone she could turn to for help was gone. Her best hope was that the Others had them. She couldn't even contemplate the idea that they were dead.

Like Ruarc.

A tear escaped. She hastily dashed it away and jumped to Ruarc's. He had it warded against the Others. At least she *hoped* it would keep them out. They would eventually find her, but she needed a few minutes to gather her thoughts and figure out what to do next.

As she moved through the penthouse, she saw Ruarc everywhere. For the briefest of moments, everything had felt right. As if she had finally found the contentment she had been waiting for. Then, it was gone in a blink, taken from her by her aunt and the Others. She had lost Ruarc, the one person who would have helped her figure a way out. She couldn't believe he was gone. Resilient, assertive, loyal Ruarc.

Another tear escaped when she recalled the look on his face when he realized that she had betrayed him. He would've forgiven her anything—except that. No matter what she had done, she would've lost—either Ruarc or her family.

"Except now, they're all gone," she said quietly.

Chevonne found herself in the doorway of Ruarc's bedroom. Her gaze latched on to the bed. It was still unmade from when Rordan had disturbed them. She'd had an entire night beside Ruarc, and she had wasted it. Hours before that, neither of them had been able to keep their hands off each other as they made love again and again.

Her heart had been full, happy. The future the brightest it had been in so very long. With one fell swoop, everything came crashing down. Chevonne felt as if she were drowning, and she didn't bother trying to swim. What was the point? The man she loved more than anything was gone. Because of her. Because of her treachery.

She hadn't even gotten to say that she was sorry or to tell him why she had done it. She needed to say those words. Chevonne rubbed the center of her chest. It ached—a profound pain that she knew would never leave.

Her gaze lifted, and she spotted the orb on his bedside table with his face flashing across it every few seconds. She strode into the room and stopped on his side of the bed. Slowly, she sank onto the mattress. Her hands shook as she reached for the orb and the message he'd left behind.

"Play," she told it.

Ruarc gazed into her eyes as he flashed a smile. *"Hello, beautiful. If you're watching this, then things didn't go as I'd hoped. You aren't alone, though. Rordan and the rest of the Reapers will be there for you. Just reach out to him. He's a good man. All of them are. Trust them. Okay?"*

He paused, his smile slipping. *"I wish I could go back in time. I never would've left you. I can't change the past, and I can't promise the future. But I've treasured every second of the present with you. You've had my heart from the first instant you grinned at me."* He chuckled and shook his head as if lost in a memory but then grew serious a moment later. *"You've always been fearless. Be fearless now. Continue spreading the word about the Others. They can't win. And remember, I may not be with you in person, but my spirit and my love will be with you always. We'll find each other in the next life and have everything we missed out on in this one. I love you."*

The recording stopped, frozen on his face as he stared at her with such love that it broke her heart. She bent forward and gave in to the flood of tears. Chevonne held the orb tighter. This was all she had left of Ruarc. She would never let it go.

She jerked at the sound of the front door being blown in. Chevonne jumped to her feet and stared at the doorway as she put the orb behind her back. In seconds, two soldiers filled the area. They looked her up and down as if she were trash. But they made no move to get to her. Blood rushed in Chevonne's ears as she waited for them to attack.

Instead, they each stepped aside. A second later, Lena walked up. Chevonne rolled her eyes as she looked away. Of course, it was her aunt.

"Did you really think I wouldn't find you?" Lena stated as if bored.

Chevonne wanted to commit every inch of Ruarc's bedroom to memory. "Fek off."

"This is the last time I'll tell you I won't tolerate such language."

Chevonne swiveled her head to her aunt. "It's no wonder your sons can't stand you."

"At least I raised my children right. More than I can say for my brother and his wife."

"Where is my family?" Chevonne demanded.

Lena smiled and crossed her arms over her chest. "Safe. I said I wouldn't kill them. I never said I wouldn't take them and ensure they do as I want."

Cold rage filled Chevonne. She took a step toward her aunt. "You think you're winning. Take this small victory while you can. Because in the end, you'll be dead, and this stupid organization you're leading will deteriorate to nothing."

"Wishful thinking," her aunt said calmly.

Chevonne smiled. "You're the one who's thinking wishfully. Do you honestly believe you can take on the Reapers and Death? Look at what they did to your soldiers today. When they come for you, *really* come for you, no amount of power you've taken from others will save you. I hope I'm there to see it."

Lena's eyes were flat. "Take her," she told the soldiers.

Chevonne jerked back as the two Fae rushed her, grabbing her arms. The orb fell from her hand. She twisted, trying to get away from the soldiers as she watched the orb bounce from the mattress and land on the rug before rolling beneath the bed. She kicked at a soldier, landing her knee in his groin.

He doubled over in pain and loosened his grip. She then shoved the heel of her palm into the other's nose. The minute she was free, she dropped down and tried to move under the bed to reach the orb. Her fingers grazed it, pushing it just out of reach. She clenched her teeth and tried to scoot farther beneath the bed, only to see the orb roll out the other side and then suddenly stop and disappear.

She stared at it for a moment before someone yanked her out by the legs. They twisted her arms painfully behind her and hauled her up before her aunt. Lena's red eyes blazed with fury.

"By the time I'm finished with you, you'll know your place," her aunt bit out.

Chevonne started to reply, but one of her arms was twisted again, causing her to cry out. In the next moment, they teleported her away.

Rordan moved his foot from the orb and bent to retrieve it as he dropped his veil. He looked across the room at Balladyn before shifting his gaze to the doorway as Cael walked in, followed by the other Reapers on his team.

"We could've stopped that," Bradach said. "All of that."

Torin shook his head. "We need the Six together, or it's pointless."

"Sooner rather than later. They've destroyed enough lives," Dubhan said.

A muscle in Cathal's jaw moved. "I vote for today."

"Patience," Cael advised, his purple gaze sliding to Rordan. "Did you get the tracker on her?"

Rordan glanced at the orb. It had been painful to watch Ruarc's last words. The way Chevonne had sought to hang onto the recording told him how much it meant to her. "Balladyn did."

"Good," Cael said with a grin.

Balladyn crossed his arms over his chest. "You think it'll work?"

"It damned well better," Rordan bit out.

Cael briefly looked at the orb in Rordan's hand. "They don't suspect her. They won't check her for any devices."

"It was wrong to keep the truth from Ruarc," Bradach said.

Dubhan grunted. "I argued against it."

"It was important that he be surprised for this to work," Cathal said.

Torin's lips curled in disgust. "It's fekking wrong."

"Because we've all been betrayed. We know that gut-wrenching feeling," Balladyn said.

The room was silent for a moment as they all became lost in thought.

Finally, Cael said, "It's time we get back."

CHAPTER SIXTEEN

No matter how much Xaneth hunted, no matter how many he took out, the evil seemed to grow. He fisted his hands as he stood atop the building and stared down at the humans and Fae walking along the sidewalks of Dublin. He'd arrived at the warehouse too late. The piles of ash told him that the Reapers had done a number on the soldiers, but he'd wanted a piece of the action.

He'd always known that evil existed. Every being on the planet did. Knowing it was there and *feeling* it were two different things, however. He didn't know why he could sense it, but he wished he could reverse it. How foolish to believe that if he sought out malevolence and vanquished it, that it would leave the realm for good.

Evil wasn't going anywhere. It couldn't. Just as good could never depart. They were joined, fused in a way that could never be severed. No matter how much anyone wanted it. It was that realization that struck Xaneth the hardest.

He couldn't ignore the reek of evil. Something within him was now wired to seek and destroy it. He was in a never-ending loop. The same kind he'd been in when Usaeil, his aunt, had tortured him. Xaneth flexed his fingers. He'd gotten out of that. He would get out of this.

Even if it meant his death.

As he swept his gaze over the crowd below, his attention lingered on long, black and silver braids. She didn't need to look up for him to know it was Aisling. He didn't know how she kept finding him, but she needed to stop. For her protection. What he was doing, the places he was going, no one needed to follow. Not even a Reaper.

She stopped suddenly. After a heartbeat, her face tilted up. Xaneth stepped back so she couldn't see him. He didn't attempt to veil himself. She'd see through it as a Reaper. After a few moments, he peered over the edge of the building, but she was gone. Thankfully. He thought about confronting her to see what she wanted. Possibly warn her to keep her distance. She had a stubbornness about her that told him she wouldn't listen to anything he had to say.

But he was getting curious as to why she tracked him. It was peculiar that no other Reapers were ever with her or pursuing him. Was Aisling on a special mission from Death? Xaneth could find out all he wanted to know simply by confronting Erith. So, why didn't he? He didn't have an answer, just a feeling in his gut. Almost as if he were programmed for one mission alone—take out evil.

He closed his eyes. Memories of his past surfaced. Free and unencumbered. He'd made his choices and developed relationships with both Light and Dark. He'd thought having to hide from Usaeil to stay alive was the worst thing he'd ever have to endure. How little he'd known. How naïve he'd been. How…gullible.

He missed that life. As hard as it had been at times. At least, he had been able to make his own decisions. Usaeil had fucked with his head and altered him. Fundamentally. He wasn't the Fae he'd once been. After his last encounter with evil, when he had taken the life of a young Dark, he didn't trust himself around anyone.

The power pulsing through his veins was unrecognizable. Once he smelled evil, he had no choice but to find and extinguish it. Whiffs of wickedness permeated the air, but it was the rancid stink of Other evil that he searched for now.

"Xaneth."

He stiffened, sensing Aisling a heartbeat before she called his name. He should teleport away. It wouldn't do any good to speak with her. That's what he told himself. Yet, he turned to her. He had no explanation for his actions.

Thick, black lashes framed her crimson eyes. She was only a few feet from him—the closest she had been yet. She had her black moto jacket unzipped, showing the silver and black shirt beneath. Dark gray jeans were tucked into black biker boots. The entire outfit told the world that she was a badass. But she didn't need clothes for that. It was in her very bearing.

"Don't leave," she said as she held out her hands in front of her in a gesture of surrender.

He drew in a breath and caught a whiff of eucalyptus—her scent. Something…peculiar… stirred deep inside him.

He needed to leave. Immediately.

"I'm going to keep following you until you talk to me," she stated.

Her deep red eyes held a challenge. One he *almost* wanted to accept. Maybe in another life, but not the one he had now. More was the pity.

"As I told the others, leave me alone," he said.

She shook her head and lowered her arms. "I can't."

"You should be with the Reapers. There was a battle with some soldiers today."

Something flashed in her eyes that she quickly banked. "If they needed me, they would have called for me."

"Would they?" he asked and lifted a brow. "Would you?"

Her gaze was steady as she held his. "What are you afraid of?"

"Nothing."

"Then why keep running from me?"

If she only knew. Xaneth didn't know what he was anymore. It was safer for every soul on the realm if he kept himself apart. At least, until someone—probably a Reaper—took his life. Maybe that's why she was here. To offer him the sweet release of death he so desperately craved. "Have you come to kill me?"

Her brows snapped together as she shot him a confused look. "What? No."

"Then why are you tracking me?"

"I…I don't really know. Call it intuition," she said with a small shrug of one shoulder.

Now that baffled him. He'd always thought Aisling a Fae who knew her mind and followed it. His curiosity became roused once more, but he banked it before it could change his mind. "You got what you wanted. You spoke with me."

"What I want is to stay with you."

The surprises kept coming. "Never going to happen."

"We're fighting the same enemy. Can't we join forces? We'd work better together. All the Reapers want you with us. As do Death and Cael."

A small part of him wanted to speak to Erith. He was pleased that she and Cael had defeated their enemy and found their love. Xaneth drew in a deep breath and released it. "No."

"No?" Aisling didn't bother hiding her anger as her crimson eyes narrowed dangerously. "Just, *no?*"

"Your hearing is excellent."

"You don't get to decide that."

He almost smiled. She had spirit, courage, and determination in spades. No wonder Erith had wanted her as a Reaper. He'd enjoyed their conversation, much to his surprise. Talking with Aisling made him feel almost…normal again. But the stench of evil—and the way something coiled and growled within him—reminded him of the monster he'd become.

"I do, actually," he whispered, right before teleporting.

~

Aisling wanted to scream. She had finally found Xaneth again, and somehow, had gotten him to talk. For a moment in their conversation, she'd thought she might convince him to let her stay, but he'd only teased her.

She swallowed as she stared at the spot he'd stood. His eyes had been sunken with dark circles around them. His skin sallow and pulled taut over his well-defined frame. Whatever he was doing, it was taking a toll. Based on what she'd seen, he couldn't handle much more. Her resolve to continue tracking him strengthened. He might not believe that he needed help, but she knew he did.

Aisling squeezed her eyes shut at the thought of her fellow Reapers fighting the soldiers. She had known that would happen when she chose to leave them to follow whatever guided her, but she didn't need to be reminded of it. Should she return to her group? Should she check in with them? As soon as the thoughts went through her head, she knew the answer—no. Come what may, she couldn't stray from Xaneth.

Death could find her if she wanted. Or force Aisling to return to the Reapers. So far, Erith had done neither. There might come a time when that happened. Until then, Aisling would remain with Xaneth. Or at least relentlessly track him. She was as surprised as he that she kept finding him.

Aisling opened her eyes and veiled herself as she walked to the edge of the building where Xaneth had stood and looked over the city. "Where did you go this time? I will find you again."

The sight of two black-clad Fae caught her attention. Soldiers. Anger simmered through her—more at herself than anyone for not being a part of the battle with her brethren earlier. She jumped from roof to roof, shadowing the soldiers. Everyone gave them a wide berth, even the humans. They strolled down the sidewalk as if they owned the city. Since the Others continued growing their ranks and power, they had no reason to think otherwise.

"Bloody wankers," Aisling murmured.

She realized they were following a trio of Light females. Aisling followed along the top of the building as the women turned down an alley, most likely to teleport. The soldiers trailed them. Aisling knelt on one knee with one hand on the roof to get a quick look at the area down below. Then she teleported behind the two soldiers.

"You'll come with us," one of the soldiers told the females.

The trio whirled around and eyed the Fae warily. "Uh…no," the middle woman answered.

Just as the soldiers lunged for her, Aisling dropped her veil and whistled as two spheres of magic formed in her palms. The soldiers pivoted around. She rolled her shoulders and shoved the orbs at them.

The soldiers both leaned to the sides. One orb missed altogether, but the other grazed the side of the soldier's face. Aisling rushed the wall and planted her foot on it, using it as leverage to jump between the soldiers and the Light females.

"Leave now!" Aisling yelled at the trio.

She didn't look behind her to see if they followed her order as the two soldiers advanced on her, throwing magic at an incredible rate. She dodged and ducked as she rushed them, lobbing her own orbs. Fighting the soldiers was a lot like training with her fellow Reapers. They were fast, skilled, and deadly.

But so was she.

She called her sword and let it move around her to attack, as well as keep the magic from landing on her. Aisling grinned as she heard one of the soldiers cry out when her blade sliced across his chest.

She used the wall once more. Only this time, a soldier grabbed her ankle and slammed her into the brick. Her head bounced against the building. Black dotted her vision. There was no way she would lose to two soldiers. She felt something slam into her wrist. The fingers holding her sword loosened, and her weapon fell away. Something warm and thick fell onto her hand. Blood. *Her* blood.

Aisling reached inside her for the rage that was always there. She let it consume her as she created a huge ball between her hands. Her blurry vision allowed her to make out the head of the soldier in front of her. She winked at him as she shoved the ball into his face.

He held her tighter, his fingers digging into her skin as he bellowed in rage and pain. The soldier's grip loosened. Aisling kicked out, trying to get free. Just before she managed it, the second soldier joined in, hurtling orbs at her in quick succession. They landed on her head, face, chest, and arms. The pain was excruciating. Worse, her vision was gone.

There was no way she would die like this. Not after everything she had survived.

Aisling shifted one hand toward the second soldier and called to her magic. The ball formed instantly. Defending against his own pain caused him to hesitate in his attack. It was the advantage she needed as she kicked free of the soldier's grip. She crashed to the ground, biting her tongue to keep in the cry of agony.

She was healing, but it would take too long to recover her eyesight enough to finish the fight. If she didn't get up now, the soldiers would kill her. She tried to get her arms under her.

Suddenly, there was a loud roar.

Aisling stilled and used her hearing. She heard scuffling around her. Grunts and harsh breathing. The unmistakable sounds of battle. But with who? Had someone else joined in? Was someone there?

Somehow, she was able to sit up. She blinked rapidly, wishing for her eyesight as she continued to listen. Then, there was silence. Aisling's heart started beating faster. If she were going to die, she would do it while standing. She flattened her hand behind her on the building and tried to get her feet under her.

"Stop. Just rest."

She relaxed when she recognized Xaneth's voice.

"I told you to stay away, dammit. What were you thinking?" he demanded furiously.

Her lips hurt to move, but she lifted her chin. "I'm a Reaper."

Xaneth sighed loudly. "I would have taken care of them if you hadn't intervened."

Her vision was beginning to return. She hadn't even known that Xaneth was there. She'd been too intent on the soldiers. All because he had told her about the earlier battle. It had been reckless and irresponsible to take on the soldiers alone.

She could just make out the outline of his head. He'd most likely saved her. "They would've killed me."

"Not likely," he replied with a snort.

Aisling blinked as her vision returned.

But Xaneth was gone.

CHAPTER SEVENTEEN

"Open your eyes."

The feminine voice was soft but insistent. The pain was finally gone. Ruarc didn't want it to return, and if he opened his eyes, it just might. He couldn't remember what had weighed so heavily upon him, but that had vanished, as well.

"Our time is short. Open your eyes, or I leave now."

Her voice wasn't so gentle now. He knew he had no choice but to obey her, though he wasn't sure why. His eyes opened. He had to blink several times to bring them into focus. When he did, a woman of incredible beauty knelt beside him. He stared into her lavender gaze. He knew her, but he wasn't sure how.

"Give it a moment," she said with a smile. "It'll all come back."

He frowned as images began moving through his head. "Death," he said as a deep pain began moving across his brow as he began to remember. "You're Death."

"I am," she replied with a sigh.

His hand came up to his chest where the orbs had entered his heart. Lena had killed him. But Chevonne had betrayed him. At the thought of her, all his memories returned. Ruarc felt the scorch marks on his shirt, but there was no wound. He looked down at his hands and flipped them palm up, but there was no blood.

He glanced around, noticing for the first time the symphony of the birds, the feel of the sunlight through the trees above him, and the heavy scent of flowers. He sat on a bed of thick grass as he reclined against a tree that towered over him. Then his gaze fell on Erith. "Where am I?"

"My realm."

Ruarc's breath caught in his throat. "Am I dead?"

"I made sure everyone in that warehouse believes you died, but I hold your soul."

"Why?" he asked worriedly.

"Only a handful are worthy of becoming a Reaper. I'm offering you an opportunity for a second life. I'll return your soul and give you additional strength and magic from my power. You will answer to me and do my bidding without question."

He studied her face, a million thoughts buzzing through his head.

"This offer doesn't last forever. It takes a lot of power to hold a soul," she warned.

Ruarc licked his lips. "I knew I was going to die."

"Your life isn't over. My Reapers have lived thousands of years longer than other Fae. What they were in their previous lives no longer mattered. Their coloring, just like yours, will remain, but you won't be Light any longer. You will heal faster, though you won't be immortal. I won't be able to save you a second time, though."

"The Others need to be stopped. I need to see that done."

She quirked an arched brow. "Is that a yes?"

How could he refuse? He knew in his bones that he had to be a part of taking the Others down for good.

"I should warn you that you won't be able to see your family," Death continued. "You will give up your former life and everyone in it."

Ruarc closed his eyes and drew in a deep breath. He'd promised his family that he would take care of them. If he agreed to become a Reaper, he would essentially be turning his back on them.

Erith asked, "May I tell you something?"

He looked at her and nodded.

"Your family is more than capable of taking care of themselves. They put it all on you because that's the type of man you are. I don't say this because I'm offering you a position as one of my Reapers. I would've told you before, but I wasn't sure you were ready to hear it."

"Either way, I'm leaving them, right?"

She nodded her head of blue-black hair. "Yes."

"Then the decision is easy."

"Is it? What about Chevonne?"

His heart clutched at the mention of her name. Her betrayal had cut deeper than anything before. Hurt worse than Lena plunging the magic into his heart. He'd believed that Chevonne was someone he could trust. He'd found out the truth. "What about her?"

"You know what I mean, Ruarc. You love her."

"She betrayed me."

"She wasn't the one who killed you."

She might as well have been, but he kept that to himself. "My answer is yes. I'll be one of your Reapers."

The instant the words were out, a surge of power rushed through him. He felt rejuvenated, invigorated. Renewed.

Erith rose to her feet. "The Reapers await your return. We have a lot of work to do. I hope you're ready for what's coming."

Ruarc stood, eager to return to the fight.

Death looked him up and down with a smile. "Just like the rest of your brethren, you were born to be a Reaper."

"You won't regret giving me this opportunity."

"I know I won't. You'll have the chance to seek your revenge on those responsible for your betrayal and death."

Ruarc was shocked at her words. He hadn't expected that. "Really?"

"I give every Reaper the opportunity."

"How many take it?"

"Does it matter?"

Ruarc shook his head. "It doesn't."

"You'll report to Eoghan for the time being since you and Rordan struck up such a friendship. We're all one family, but the Reapers are divided into two groups for now."

"And going forward?" he pushed.

That slow, secretive smile of hers graced her face. "We'll have to see, won't we? Now, come. Rordan is eager to see you. As are the rest."

Ruarc followed her through a maze of flowers to the Fae doorway. After he stepped through it, he found himself on a small isle.

"This is Scotland," Erith told him. "No one would think to look for a doorway for us here."

He chuckled as he turned in a circle to remember the location. "No, they would not."

Once he faced her again, she grinned and vanished. He blinked in stunned silence. Had she told him where to go, and he didn't hear? Was this some test? Where was she?

Ruarc drew in a breath and released it to calm himself. He closed his eyes. He was a Reaper now. He had additional powers that he knew nothing about. Yet, as he remained still and quiet, he felt the Earth. The hum of magic low and constant, the heartbeats of billions of living souls, and the feeling of a different kind of power—Reaper power.

His eyes snapped open as he found his brethren. Ruarc teleported to the tunnels beneath Dublin. The sound of dripping water and a stale scent permeated the air around him. A warm, amber glow filled the space. His gaze swept the arched chamber and the Reapers. Ruarc looked to Erith first.

She shrugged. "I knew you'd find us."

"Welcome to our esteemed group," Cael said as he bowed his head. "I'm Cael."

Ruarc returned the nod, noting how Cael and Erith stood close together.

Rordan stepped forward. There was a hint of sadness in his

gaze. "You're going to fit in perfectly. Fianna wished to be here, but she sends her regards. Fi and Neve are guarding your family."

"Is Fi one of us?" Ruarc asked.

Rordan smiled slowly and nodded. "She is."

"If the way you fought earlier is any indication, I'd say you were born for this," said a white-haired Reaper. "I'm Fintan."

Ruarc's eyes widened in surprise. Was he really standing in front of the infamous assassin? "I always thought you were a myth."

Fintan smiled as his red-ringed white eyes crinkled at the corners. "I think everyone would like to believe I'm not real."

"Oh, he's real," Daire said with a roll of his silver eyes.

One by one, the group introduced themselves.

Balladyn was last as he flashed a grin. "You had a calling in the Light army, but I'm glad to have you with us."

Ruarc glanced around at the incredible group he was with. Just as Erith had said, they'd retained their coloring. Light and Dark Fae milled together, but there wasn't the same tension that usually accompanied such a gathering. Erith had told him that he was no longer Light. He was a Reaper. Just as the others around him were. They got to shake off their former lives and everything that defined them to become something more.

Cael clasped his hands behind his back. "There's little time for you to get a handle on your new powers."

"I'll figure it out," Ruarc said.

Dubhan's red eyes crinkled as he said, "We're all thrown into things at first."

"How long can I stay veiled?" Ruarc asked.

Kyran shrugged as he crossed his arms over his chest. "As long as you want."

He smiled. "Seriously?"

"Try it," Torin urged.

Ruarc veiled himself. A few moments later, several other Reapers did. He could still see them, which meant they could see him. There was a shimmery look about them. He dropped his veil. "You look different with your veil up," he told Rordan.

"I do?" Rordan looked down at himself then chuckled. "I've been a Reaper so long, I forgot how Fae look with their veils up."

Bradach shook his head as he smiled. "We can see any veiled Fae. No one but another Reaper, Erith, and Cael, can see a Reaper with his or her veil up."

It was good knowledge. Ruarc couldn't wait to find out what else he could do.

"It's time to get started," Erith said.

For so long, Ruarc had worked alone. It felt odd at first to be part of a group, but it didn't take long for him to find his way. Erith might rule the Reapers, but she not only welcomed everyone's input, she wanted it.

Ruarc had very little to offer at the moment. No one pushed him, either. He was finding his footing. While he had gotten a second chance at life, it would be a much different one. Everyone was giving him time to adjust.

For over an hour, they debated how to get to the Six.

"We can fight the soldiers for eternity, and it won't make a difference," Eoghan stated.

Dubhan's lips curled into a sneer. "Not when the Six keep making more."

"Just as Erith makes Reapers," Baylon pointed out as his gaze landed on Ruarc.

Suddenly, everyone looked his way. Ruarc had his arms crossed over his chest as he shrugged.

"Not as easily," Death pointed out.

Cael shook his head. "Erith has high standards for those she chooses as her Reapers."

"The highest," she said as she gazed up at him with adoration.

An image of Chevonne's face filled Ruarc's mind. He shoved it aside. She had made her choice. He'd fallen for her lies and had paid the highest price. The best thing he could do was forget that she ever meant anything to him. It wasn't as if he had a choice. He'd agreed to give up everything from his old life. That included Chevonne.

"Can I talk to you?"

Ruarc jerked, brought out of his musing. He glanced around to see that the others had moved away. When Rordan turned on his heel and walked off, Ruarc followed. Rordan continued down the darkened tunnel and didn't stop until they were out of earshot of the others.

Rordan snapped his fingers, and that same warm, amber glow from the other room presented itself above them. Rordan's face was lined with concern. "There are things you need to know."

"I'm listening."

Rordan shifted feet, his agitation palpable. "Balladyn stayed behind at your flat earlier with Chevonne."

Ruarc's abdomen clenched, the sound of Chevonne's name like a punch to his gut. He didn't want to know. Nothing Rordan said would make a difference. Yet he found himself asking, "And?"

"We noticed her distress. We made a split-second decision for him to remain behind and make sure everything was fine."

"Do the two of you always go in pairs with one veiled?"

Rordan's shoulders lifted as he sucked in a breath. "In times like these when we have to make sure soldiers aren't watching, aye."

"Are you going to tell me what Balladyn saw?" Ruarc didn't want to know. But no matter how many times he told himself that, he couldn't make it true. He must like the torture. There was no other reason for him to ask that question.

Rordan's throat moved as he swallowed. "She called for her aunt. That's when Chevonne told her where we were going to meet and set the trap for the soldiers."

"And where she told Lena there were ten Reapers. I gave her that number."

"Yes."

Ruarc nodded, feeling empty inside. "I never suspected Chevonne of anything. I wanted so desperately to believe that she had returned because she loved me. That it wasn't just coincidence that she came back into my life now."

"There's more."

Ruarc ran his hand through his hair. "Fek me. Do I need to hear any more?"

"I think you do."

"Fine," Ruarc said with a resigned sigh. "Just spit it all out."

Rordan paused for a moment until Ruarc looked at him. Then the Reaper said, "Lena threatened Chevonne's family as well as you if she didn't comply. It seems that as long as Chevonne didn't tell you about Lena's plans, she would allow you to live. Chevonne tried to get away, but Lena took her to the warehouse."

No. No, that simply wasn't possible. "Lena was at the party. That's where she confronted Chevonne. I told Chevonne that the Six never left their compound."

"You couldn't know her aunt was the leader of the Six."

"I knew Lena looked familiar." Ruarc balled his hands into fists. "I wish I would've recognized her soon."

"Lena made sure you felt as if you had nowhere to turn for help. No doubt she did the same, if not more, to Chevonne since you were working with us. The way she stared at Chevonne makes me think that Lena has plans for her. Balladyn agreed after what he witnessed between them."

Ruarc's knees began to wobble. He couldn't breathe. He shifted, reaching out and grasping hold of the wall to keep himself upright. It was easier when he thought Chevonne had betrayed him. Now, knowing the truth, things were much worse. "This can't be happening."

"Everyone gave up our past to be a Reaper. I know what you're feeling. At least now, you can do something to help Chevonne."

"I just can't be with her." Ruarc turned his head to look at Rordan.

Rordan couldn't meet his gaze.

"You have Fi," Ruarc said. "Other Reapers have mates. Is there a chance…?" He couldn't finish the sentence.

Rordan shrugged. "That's between you and Erith."

This was worse than death. "Did Erith know all of this when she asked me to be a Reaper?"

"Yes," Rordan admitted.

Ruarc straightened and dropped his head back as rage and the bitter taste of resentment overwhelmed him.

"We need you. You're a born fighter, Ruarc. You went up against those soldiers and held your own as a Fae. Imagine what you can do as a Reaper."

It wasn't as if Ruarc had many choices. He could stayed dead and never known how anything turned out. Or…he could take a stand alongside those who were doing the right thing.

He looked at Rordan. The Reaper held up his hand with the orb that held the recording he'd made for Chevonne.

"She got away from Lena briefly. We suspected someone might go to your flat. While Erith had you, the rest of us waited at your penthouse," Rordan said. "Chevonne showed up first. She was visibly distraught. She found your recording and watched it. It wasn't long after that Lena and some soldiers arrived. They didn't even try to see if any Reapers were there. They focused on Chevonne." Rordan held out the orb. "She tried to hold onto it, but they knocked it from her hand."

Ruarc took the orb and held it against him. "What happened to Chevonne?"

"They took her."

"And you did nothing?" he bellowed.

Rordan gave him a flat look. "They're holding her family. They don't plan on harming her. They want something from her."

Cold fury drummed through Ruarc. "I may not be able to be with Chevonne, but I won't allow her to be Lena's puppet."

"None of us will. That's why we put a tracker on her."

Ruarc walked away. Fury filled him so completely he could hardly breathe. Lena would know the full ire of a Reaper.

By the time Ruarc was finished with her, there would be nothing left.

CHAPTER EIGHTEEN

"Don't bother trying to fight the inevitable. I'll do whatever it takes to break you."

Lena's parting words hadn't frightened Chevonne. They'd pissed her off. She refused to shed the tears that burned her eyes. How had Lena hidden who she truly was all this time? How had no one seen it? She didn't know what her aunt had planned, but it didn't matter. She would fight whatever it was.

She paced the large, beautiful room, though she didn't notice any of the fine furnishings. Hate and loathing threatened to swallow her whole. She had already tried to bust through the windows—as well as the door—but she hadn't been able to get through. She wasn't even sure she had magic anymore since nothing she tried worked to free her. If she did, it wasn't making a dent. And no one was answering her summons.

Chevonne turned and slammed her hands against the wall. She wanted to scream her anger at her predicament and bellow her sorrow for the loss of Ruarc. Never had she imagined that Lena would kill him. She had actually believed that Lena would hold up her end of the bargain. But the proof was in her aunt's now-red eyes.

The soldiers around Lena hadn't blinked at the change of color. Chevonne wondered if it mattered since Lena was one of the three Light Fae. Technically, she was no longer Light. Would that change the dynamic of the Six? Chevonne had a sinking feeling that Lena wouldn't give up any position. Ever.

Chevonne pushed away from the wall. She didn't know where her family was or even if they were alive. She could only speculate about what Lena had in store for all of them. Chevonne loved her family, and she didn't want to see any of them harmed, but she couldn't—*wouldn't*— give in to Lena's demands.

It was one thing to pass information along to keep her family safe. But that was as far as she would go. She had drawn a figurative line in the sand.

"*I'll do whatever it takes to break you.*"

Unfortunately, Chevonne suspected that her aunt would indeed keep her promise. It was easy for Chevonne to state all kinds of things while alone in the lavishly appointed room, but when faced with something, would she stand her ground?

"Ruarc would," she whispered.

He wouldn't cross that imaginary line in the sand. The only way she could get through whatever came next was to visualize Ruarc beside her. He'd told her in the recording that his spirit would walk with her always. She needed him. Desperately.

What she wouldn't do to see him once more. To wrap her arms around him and feel his strength. To hear his laughter or see the desire in his eyes. He was the best Fae she knew. And she had betrayed him. She'd thought she was protecting him, but she should've known. She should've guessed what her aunt planned.

Chevonne squeezed her eyes closed as she recalled the look of anguish on Ruarc's face. Shame choked her. The tears she had battled against won as a single drop escaped her lids and rolled down her cheek. She angrily wiped it away. She couldn't show any kind of weakness. Lena would pounce on it.

If only she were strong enough to withstand whatever was coming. But Chevonne wasn't sure she could. Her heart was shattered at the loss of Ruarc. It was bad enough that she had betrayed him, but watching him die had been the worst experience of her life.

That wouldn't be all her aunt did. Lena wanted to break her. For what purpose, though? What could be so important that her aunt would go to such trouble to get her and the rest of the family? Chevonne leaned against the wall and tried to think back through anything that might give her a clue as to why Lena was so intent on their family.

She had no idea how long she stood there going through her memories when the door to her room swung open. Chevonne pushed away from the wall, but she didn't go toward the entry. No doubt this was some kind of trick.

"Clara? Are you here?"

The sound of her father's voice propelled her out of the room. Chevonne halted in the corridor and looked right, then left. She saw her father peeking his head around another door.

"Da," she called.

His head swung to her. "Chevonne," he said as he rushed to her.

She ran to him and threw her arms around him. It felt so good to be in his arms. She fought against the tide of tears. She had so much to tell him, but she didn't know where to begin. "Oh, Da."

"Are you okay?" he asked in a shaky voice.

She leaned back enough to look at him. Her father had always been strong and hale, but he looked aged now. She clung to the fact that he was alive. "I'm fine. What of Mum, Eileen, and Shannon?"

"I've not seen them since we were taken."

"When? What happened?" she pushed since she didn't know how long they had.

Her father's face creased heavily with apprehension. "At the party. Light and Dark Fae dressed in all black invaded the house. They began snatching people. I looked for you, but I couldn't find you."

"I left to return to Ruarc." While her family and others were attacked. Lena had waited until she was gone to strike. Chevonne felt sick to her stomach.

Her father's silver eyes darted around her. "I know your mother was taken. I saw it. I'm not sure about your sisters."

"She said she had them."

"She?" her father asked, his frown deepening.

Chevonne swallowed, not wanting to tell him. He was already so distraught. This might send him over the edge. "Aunt Lena."

"No," he said and jerked back. "She's not part of this."

"She's the leader of the Others, Da. Head of the Six."

He shook his head. "I know my sister. She might be taciturn at times, but she would never do this to her family."

"She forced me to do what she wanted with the promise that she wouldn't harm any of you. I didn't know she would take you prisoner. She killed Ruarc."

"Impossible," he stated. As if that alone proved she was wrong.

Chevonne's heart broke for him. Hugo Quinlan was a good man, and he loved his family dearly. She'd always believed he was strong mentally and physically. Now, she saw for the first time that everyone had a breaking point. Her father had reached his sometime after the attack at the party.

"Whatever Lena wants, don't give in," Chevonne whispered.

He shook his head. "Enough. That's your aunt."

"That's what I keep telling her."

Chevonne stiffened at the sound of Lena's voice behind her. She should've known her aunt would set this up. Chevonne slowly turned to face her, though she didn't release her father.

"Lena," Hugo said with a smile. "I'm so glad you're here. I don't know where Chevonne has gotten these wild ideas about you."

Lena said nothing until she drew close enough for Hugo to see her eyes.

"Wh-what?" he asked in shock. "Is this some joke?"

Lena shook her head. "Not at all."

"Chevonne spoke the truth, then? You killed Ruarc?" he asked hesitantly.

Lena shrugged as she glanced at Chevonne. "Ruarc fell in with a bad crowd and was going to harm Chevonne. I had to do something."

"She's lying," Chevonne stated.

Hugo looked between the two of them, doubt hardening his features.

Chevonne glared at Lena. "What's your end game? What do you want with all of us?"

"Perhaps you should be asking what is happening to your mother and sisters," Lena said with a smile.

Fear snaked its cold hand down Chevonne's spine. "Where are they? We had a deal."

"That deal is finished."

Chevonne had never wanted to harm anyone until that moment. "You're a liar. You will twist anyone's words to what you want."

"Because I can see the truth no one else can." Lena shrugged. "You will soon enough, though. Once I have your little family where I want them, there won't be anything the Reapers can do to stop me."

Chevonne's heart dropped like lead to her feet. She gripped her father tightly, needing someone to hold onto.

Lena rolled her eyes. "Don't look so stricken. You'll be much happier in the end. It's going to turn out how it should have long ago."

"What are you talking about?" Hugo asked, finding his voice.

Her aunt swung her gaze to her brother. "Don't you remember when we found our family lineage hidden in the attic of Grandmother's house? We saw the undeniable proof of who we are. No one will be able to refute that or refuse me. It's my destiny."

"What of the Six?" Chevonne asked. Lena had been talking about herself for some time and leaving out the rest of her group that helped to put her in power.

She shrugged. "What of them?"

"I don't think they'll take kindly to whatever you have planned. Or how you're now a Dark."

Lena smiled deviously. "There's a lot they don't know."

Chevonne glanced at her father when he tightened his grip on her hand. Given the pallor of his skin, the truth was beginning to sink in.

"Lena, where are Clara, Eileen, and Shannon?" he demanded.

"Come. I'll show you," she replied with a smirk as she turned and walked away.

Chevonne knew they shouldn't follow her. Lena had some other trick planned, but she had to see her mother and sisters.

"We shouldn't go," her father whispered.

She met his gaze. "I know. But we have to."

"Promise me that you'll do whatever you have to in order to stay alive."

"We're all going to leave here together."

He patted her hand and smiled ruefully. "We both know that isn't going to happen."

CHAPTER NINETEEN

Ruarc wanted to hit something. No, he wanted to fight. He needed to find the soldiers—or Lena—and take out everything he felt on them. It was the only way he'd be able to breathe freely again.

When he returned to the other Reapers, he could tell by the looks they gave him that everyone had known about Chevonne. Everyone, that is, except him.

"You all knew."

"I wanted to be the one to tell you," Rordan answered. "I felt I owed you that."

Ruarc looked at the ground as he attempted to rein in his anger. He finally gave up and lifted his head. "Tell me we aren't waiting to attack."

"We aren't," Eoghan replied.

Cael crossed his arms over his chest. "The plan we discussed earlier is part of us going after the Six now."

"I assume this has to do with the tracker you put on Chevonne?" Ruarc asked.

Fintan's lips flattened before he said, "The Six have a way of hiding from even Erith. We had to resort to other measures."

Ruarc was impressed. "Smart thinking. If they don't check her."

"They didn't at your flat," Cathal told him.

Erith's lavender gaze landed on him. "Based on the intel we have, we think Lena has something planned for Chevonne and the rest of the family. Including Lena's own son."

Ruarc shook his head as he tried to think what that could be. "For what reason? Chevonne's family is well known and has tremendous clout, but they're not special in any other way."

"They must be. Why else would Lena break rank with the Six to take them?" Cael asked.

Kyran made a noise in the back of his throat. "My mate, River, can read obscure Fae languages. She's the warden of books from the original Fae families."

"In other words," Talin said with a look at Kyran, "River is checking the books to see if there's something about Chevonne's family."

Ruarc shrugged and shook his head. "The Quinlans are above reproach."

Balladyn's face suddenly creased into a deep frown. "Quinlan?"

"What is it?" Ruarc asked.

The former King of the Dark looked from Ruarc to Erith. "I remember the name from a book in my library."

"Do you recall what it said about them?" Rordan asked.

Balladyn shook his head. "Not off the top of my head. I need the book."

"Get it," Erith ordered. "Kyran, go with him and bring River. Talin, you, Rordan, and Cathal check on Neve and Fi as well as Ruarc's family. If it appears they're safe, bring the girls here while Cathal makes sure the Druids return to Skye."

Cael flashed a smile at his mate. "If we're going to strike, let's end things now."

Erith whispered something to Cael before vanishing. Ruarc watched as Kyran, Balladyn, Talin, and Rordan teleported away. He fisted his hands. He was restless and impatient. Edgy. He wanted to battle the soldiers again.

No. He wanted Lena. He wanted to rip her head from her body. She, as leader of the Six, had instigated all of this. Even if she hadn't formed the Others, she had been instrumental in gathering the Fae and producing soldiers.

"It'll come soon enough," Fintan said as he moved to stand beside him.

Ruarc never thought himself bloodthirsty before. But he was now. "Not quick enough."

"It doesn't matter how many of the enemy you kill. It doesn't stop the pain."

Eoghan leaned back against the tunnel wall. "Fintan's right. The pain will still be there when the battle is over."

"You might feel a little better in the heat of it, but it won't last," Cael added.

Ruarc looked at his new family. He wanted to ask them how they had become Reapers, but he couldn't get the words out.

Fintan raised a white brow. "You may not know, but every Reaper Erith brings to this group has exceptional battle skills. We were all also betrayed and murdered."

Ruarc's lips parted in dismay.

"Which means we know exactly how you feel," Cael said.

Eoghan shrugged. "The difference is, we didn't turn around and fight those responsible for our demise."

"Did none of you seek revenge?" he finally asked.

Baylon's lips twisted. "We all thought about it."

"A few of us have taken our revenge," Torin said.

Dubhan rolled his eyes. "What we're trying to say is that you have a chance none of us had. Take it. We have your back, just as we know you have ours."

"Just don't hold onto the anger once the battle is over—win or lose," Bradach cautioned. "It'll twist you into something you aren't."

As Ruarc looked at each of them, he realized that they had all been aware of his betrayal. And they had all witnessed his death. "Did you know I'd become a Reaper? Is that why no one told me about the betrayal?"

"Only Erith knows those she watches to be Reapers," Cael answered. "No one told you about Chevonne because we needed you to act shocked. If we'd have known Lena intended to kill you, we would've stopped it."

"It doesn't matter if you knew or not." Ruarc smiled at them to show he meant it. "I was chained by obligations to my family. I'm free of that responsibility now."

Eoghan's liquid-silver eyes held his. "You aren't free of the love you hold for Chevonne."

"I'll deal with that," he stated.

Fintan snorted loudly. "Denial isn't a good look on you."

"Isn't it better to think like that than believe I can be with her?" he asked.

Before anyone had time to answer, Balladyn returned with a stack of books. A wooden table appeared before him, right as he set the pile down. A moment later, Kyran returned with another armload. Next to him, holding more books, was a woman with long, straight, dark brown hair and pale blue eyes.

She flashed a smile at Ruarc. "I'm River. Welcome to the family."

"Hi," Ruarc replied, a little stunned by her warm greeting.

River didn't have Fae coloring, but she was beautiful. The fact that she could read ancient Fae languages of the original families meant that she was a Halfling.

Ruarc watched as she motioned to where she wanted Kyran to space out the books from one side of the table. Balladyn was on the other as he sped-read his way through book after book. Ruarc had known comradery in the army, but this was different. In the Light army, he'd fought for the queen and the Light. As a Reaper, he fought for all Fae—and for the realm.

It wasn't long before Talin returned. A Light with long, black hair plaited down her back and silver eyes stood dressed for battle beside him.

She walked from Talin and stopped before Ruarc. "I'm sorry for what brought you here, but I'm glad to have you with us. I'm Neve, by the way."

"Ruarc," he replied.

She stepped aside just as Rordan and Fianna appeared. In two strides, Fi was before him, her arms around his neck. "I'm so, so sorry," she whispered.

"Thanks," Ruarc said and gave her a quick squeeze.

Fianna blinked rapidly as she stepped away. "The other mates are anxious to meet you."

Ruarc smiled since he didn't know what to say. He wasn't sure he would make it past this battle. He hoped he did because the idea of being part of something so great gave him a sense of purpose he hadn't felt in a very long time.

Cathal returned. "The Druids are back on Skye."

He hadn't finished speaking when Erith returned. Her gaze went to River first. "Anything?"

"Not yet," River said as she continued reading.

Balladyn lowered the book in his hand. "I knew I'd read the Quinlan name."

"What did you find?" Erith asked, her lavender eyes laser-focused on him.

Ruarc's heart began to pump hard in his chest. He wasn't sure if he wanted to know what Balladyn had found or not because he couldn't shake the thought that it wasn't good.

Balladyn glanced his way. "This book is the only edition. It was written by a Fae who worked with those changing names. She talks about one name she wasn't supposed to keep a record of, but she did anyway. Two hundred thousand years ago, a family took the name of Quinlan. It was to hide the fact that they were previously Muldowney."

The tunnel went silent as everyone took that in. There wasn't a Light or Dark alive who didn't know that name. It held the same connotations as Hitler or Stalin.

"Fek me," Fintan murmured.

River laid her palms flat on the table and read, "*The Muldowneys reach for power has nearly undone everything the Fae have forged. Their solitary purpose has been to rule all, but we knew they would never stop there. We had no choice but to eradicate them before they destroyed our planet and the Fae.*" River glanced up and said, "There's a sidenote. All of them were killed except for a young lad and an infant boy. The group decided that the children were young enough not to know their family or the machinations they were involved in. They were given a new name."

Erith's brow furrowed as she stared at the wall. "The secret wasn't kept. Someone had to have told the boys."

"Lena found out about her ancestry," Ruarc said. "She must have."

Cael blew out a slow breath. "The Muldowneys' magic rivaled that of the royals. They studied magic and how to increase their power. Some remained Light, while others turned Dark, but one goal unified them."

"To rule the Fae," Eoghan said.

Erith lifted her chin. "Now we have a Muldowney descendant trying to do what her ancestors couldn't."

"Except she's gathering power and becoming stronger than her ancestors," Neve pointed out.

Ruarc ran his hand over his jaw. "We know what we're up against now. We know what the end goal is. Lena doesn't care about the Others. She wants to rule, and she's going to attempt it."

"There has to be a reason she needed Chevonne and the others in her family," Fianna pointed out.

Balladyn snorted. "Because the more of those with the same blood around, the more powerful she'll be."

"Especially if she takes their magic," Rordan added.

It felt as if a building were pressing on Ruarc's chest. He couldn't breathe. Could barely think past the fact that Lena planned to kill Chevonne.

"We need to go," Cael said.

Erith looked around the room, her gaze stopping at Ruarc. "I need everyone focused and calm. The Others sent soldiers after us, and they will continue as long as the organization is functioning. If we don't act as a group, we falter. And they win."

"I won't let you down," Ruarc said.

Fintan slapped him on the back. "We never thought you would."

"Let's go!" Eoghan said.

The Reapers teleported away, one by one. Kyran grasped River when he left.

Rordan walked to Ruarc and said, "Follow our magic. Can you see it?"

Ruarc blinked, shocked that he could see the ribbons of magic making a trail. Then he was alone. Anticipation surged through him as he teleported and followed the magic. In the next heartbeat, he stood veiled with the Reapers outside of a castle perched on a cliff. Kyran returned alone and nodded to Erith.

Fianna and Rordan were the first to walk toward the castle. Within a few steps, Fi fell to her knees, her lips pulled back in agony. Rordan's hands were fisted, his face mottled with pain. He stepped back and dragged Fi with him.

"Fekking Reaper wards," Rordan said as his chest heaved.

Erith lifted her gaze to the castle. "I can take care of that."

"We both will," Cael stated.

Ruarc almost felt sorry for anyone that ran into Cael and Erith. Then he remembered Chevonne and her betrayal, and he couldn't wait to join the goddess and god.

CHAPTER TWENTY

Chevonne might have enjoyed what little she saw of the castle if panic and animosity weren't choking her. She glared at her aunt's back, wishing she could strike her. As if reading her mind, her father squeezed her hand.

She didn't want to show him how scared she was. Just as he tried not to let on about his apprehension. But there was no denying it. Chevonne wanted to reassure her father that they would get out of this alive. The words, however, never made it past her lips. She wouldn't appreciate it if he lied to her. She wouldn't do that to him. They were both intelligent adults. They could see what was coming.

"I'll never forgive her if she's done something to your mum and sisters," her father whispered.

Tears gathered in Chevonne's eyes. Her family had always been important to her. She had done what she needed to keep them safe. Or she thought she had. Lena hadn't given her all the facts. Then again, when did a soul-sucking, malicious bitch spill their plans? Never.

Chevonne had been duped multiple times by Lena. Everyone in the Others had. She suspected even those in the Six. A vengeful part of her wanted to witness it when everyone else learned of Lena's true ambition. That wouldn't happen. All Chevonne could hope for now was that her death would be painless and quick. Knowing her aunt, that probably wouldn't happen.

They walked into a large room that might have been a ballroom at one time. Chevonne had expected to see Others or the Six. Instead, she spotted a small group of soldiers surrounding her mother, Eileen, Shannon, Cillian, and her uncle, all of which were seated.

"Clara," her father said when he saw his wife.

Her mother's gaze briefly met his, but she quickly looked away. As if seeing him would break her. Eileen stared at Chevonne, and she had a feeling her sister was trying to tell her something. Chevonne's gaze moved to Shannon, but her middle sister stared at the floor, refusing to look up.

Fear hung like a shroud in the room. It was on the tip of Chevonne's tongue to call out for Rordan. Would he answer her summons? Could he even get in? Did she dare try? She was willing to do anything to save her family. Hadn't she already betrayed the one person she'd never thought to hurt in any way for them?

A sob lodged in her throat. She had to work her mouth twice before she was able to say, "Rordan."

Lena chuckled as she stopped in the middle of the room and faced her. "Do you think I'd be stupid enough to allow Reapers in here? We have wards to prevent the Reapers' entry. Panic breeds desperation, and you don't wear despair well, my dear."

"Enough, Lena," Chevonne's father said in a firm voice. "It's time you tell me what all of this is."

Lena rolled her eyes and sighed. "You never did listen well, Hugo. I've already told you."

Chevonne watched his face harden. "This is about our family lineage."

"We've hidden for long enough. Our ancestors had the right idea. I'm carrying through with that," Lena said with an evil tilt her lips.

"What have you done, sister?" Hugo asked, anger dripping from his words.

Lena laughed and clasped her hands before her. "I used to hate how everyone fawned over you, Hugo. How intelligent you were, how amiable. How charming. Our parents constantly told me to smile more, to be friendlier. I was never good enough for them. I always felt like such an outsider in our family. Turns out, I'm the only one who truly fits in."

The more Chevonne listened, the more her anxiety grew. As far as she knew, the Quinlans had a great reputation among the Fae— and even the humans. What could possibly be in their history that had set Lena off?

"You were supposed to have burned that family tree," her father stated.

Lena shot him an exasperated look. "Why would I? The truth was there for everyone to see. Just saying the name strikes fear in the hearts of all Fae."

There was only one name that could do that. Chevonne's gut twisted at the thought of being related to the Muldowneys.

"That's right," Lena said with a laugh. She walked closer to Chevonne. "All of us are descendants of the Muldowneys. Do you have any idea the power that runs through our veins?"

"Whatever you plan, you'll never succeed," Chevonne said.

Lena's brows rose on her forehead. "Because of the Reapers? Because of the Dragon Kings?" A cruel smile curved her lips. "By the time I'm finished tonight, *no one* will be able to stop me."

That's when Chevonne realized that Lena intended to take all their magic, killing them in the process. Ice ran through her veins as her heart slammed erratically against her ribs. Her hands were clammy as she gripped her father and struggled to draw breath.

Lena smiled at Hugo, then at Clara. "Thank you for having your party. It made it so easy to get everyone. Cillian proved to be a bit of an issue, but I won in the end. I always win." Lena looked at Chevonne. "Thanks to Chevonne, I was able to get close to the Reapers and kill Ruarc. He was a pain, and to be honest, my dear, he wasn't up to our family's standards. I am disappointed in you. Oscar was a much better option."

"You know nothing," Chevonne said.

Her aunt laughed, shrugging. "Imagine my surprise when I learned you found your way back to Ruarc. That allowed me to use both of you to my advantage. It couldn't have worked out better had I planned it."

"The way I see it, the Reapers won today. They destroyed your soldiers," Chevonne said tightly.

Lena slowly shook her head. "To think I considered making you my protégé. You were always so clever—or so I thought. I'm glad I changed my mind."

"What did you do to the Reapers?" Chevonne demanded.

Her father pulled her back against him. She was so furious, she hadn't realized she had moved toward her aunt.

Lena's gaze raked over her in disdain. "I always thought the Fae were powerful beings. Turns out, we haven't even begun to tap into the power that awaits us. That's what my Muldowney ancestors did. They learned how to grow their magic. The more power I have, the more magic I'm able to do. So many wonderful things opened to me and the rest of the Six."

"But you grew greedy," her father said.

Lena lifted one shoulder in a shrug. "Why should I share? If I have it all to myself, then I don't have to bicker with anyone over what I know is the best course of action for our kind."

"What. Did. You. Do?" Chevonne repeated.

Lena's lips curled cruelly. "Every time a soldier drew blood from a Reaper, I took some of their magic."

Chevonne's legs nearly gave out. That couldn't possibly be true. It just...couldn't.

"The soldiers you see here have just a sip of what I gained earlier. So, when it comes time for me to take out the Six, my soldiers will easily wipe everyone out. They may not be able to go up against the Reapers or Death, or even the Dragon Kings, but I'll be able to handle that."

Her father shook his head, contempt twisting his face. "You've lost your mind."

"No, Hugo, I've found it!" she snapped.

Ruarc fanned out with the others in the ballroom, listening to everything. Lena was so confident that the Reapers couldn't get into the castle that she didn't have her soldiers searching for them. Ruarc liked being able to remain veiled for as long as he wanted. It was just too bad they couldn't make a sound lest they be heard.

He glanced at the rest of the Reapers. After Erith and Cael had easily walked through the wards and erased them, the Reapers swept through the castle. They hadn't attacked any soldiers—yet. They needed to find Chevonne and Lena first.

At the sight of Chevonne, Ruarc's heart nearly burst with happiness at finding her still alive. They had arrived in time. He wanted to drop his veil so her gaze could find him, but he knew it was impossible. The plan was for him to remain veiled during the entire battle. Lena couldn't learn that he was a Reaper in case she managed to survive the battle. He was Erith's ace in the hole.

Still, he had to fight not to go to Chevonne. He wanted her to know that he was alive and that he forgave her. He should've known that she would never betray him without a good reason. If he could, he would make it up to her. Maybe it was better if he was out of her life forever. Ruarc would make sure she lived. That way, she could make a fresh start. She wouldn't be weighed down by her past with him. Their love, hopes, and dreams would have to wait for another life.

It would be painful to see her move on, but he loved her enough to want her happy. Even if it was without him.

As for him, he would love her for eternity. There was no other for him.

"Who's first?" Lena asked in a hard voice as she looked from Chevonne and Hugo to the rest of the family.

Lena's husband, Colm, stepped forward. "If you must do this, then take me. But leave our son alone."

She gave Colm a smile filled with love before she burst out laughing. "Don't worry, sweetheart. You will die tonight, but you won't be first. You aren't a Muldowney, which means you don't really have the magic I want. That doesn't mean I won't take yours, however."

A stricken look crossed his face. "Please leave our son out of it."

"He has what I need. I'll have more children later if I want. Though to be honest, I doubt that will be the case," she said with an indifferent shrug.

Ruarc saw Chevonne and Eileen exchange a long look. The two sisters were planning something. Even though they knew they would be beaten, they were still going to take a stand. Ruarc smiled at his courageous love.

Eoghan caught his attention from across the room. The Reapers, Erith, and Cael had also noticed the exchange between the sisters. Ruarc nodded as he realized they were going to wait until the sisters attacked before they launched their own assault.

Erith held out her hand, and the same black sword he'd seen during their last battle appeared in her palm. Even the blade was black. Some Reapers formed magic in each hand. Others had orbs in one hand and weapons in the other.

Ruarc called his sword. It had cost him a pretty penny, but he'd been willing to pay it. The army supplied weapons, but everyone knew if you wanted to survive the war, you needed a blade forged in the Fires of Erwar. A Fae could heal from a wound inflicted by a regular weapon, but not one made in Erwar.

His attention slid to Chevonne as she stepped away from her father and shoved Lena so hard she went flying across the floor. The fact that Chevonne hadn't used magic surprised everyone but Ruarc. Chevonne always had a knack for doing the unexpected.

Eileen and Shannon jumped to their feet and began hurling spheres of magic at Lena. Cillian, Hugo, and Clara joined them. Just as the soldiers moved to stop the attack, all but Ruarc dropped their veils and joined in the fray.

Ruarc spun toward the two soldiers behind him. He plunged his sword into one's chest. He exploded into ash instantly. The second slid to a halt and used the spell to force Ruarc's veil down. But he had expected as much and moved before the magic could hit him. He came up behind the soldier and beheaded him.

Ruarc's gaze scanned the room for Chevonne. Once he saw that she was holding her own, he looked for Lena. The Six's leader was on her feet, violence pouring off her as she formed a huge orb and set to hurtle it at Chevonne.

"No!" Hugo bellowed as he rushed in front of Chevonne before the magic could hit her.

Instead of killing him, the sphere held him immobile and began sizzling with electricity jumping off it. White mist gathered above him and flowed from Hugo to Lena. By the time Ruarc realized that Lena had taken her brother's magic, he was dead.

Ruarc took a step toward her when he spotted Balladyn battling five soldiers. Lena would have to wait. He rushed to Balladyn and sliced a soldier from throat to groin.

CHAPTER TWENTY-ONE

Building after building, Xaneth searched for evil. True evil. The kind he was meant to find. But it seemed just out of reach. As if it knew that he chased it and stayed one step ahead of him.

Worse, Aisling had somehow managed to find him quicker than usual. She was always there, waiting to catch up. She said she needed to be with him, but he knew the best thing she could do was get as far away as possible. Still, the woman was stubborn. She refused to listen.

Or leave.

What compelled him was too strong to ignore or attempt to explain. He couldn't find words to describe it to himself. He only knew that he had to seek out the evil and destroy it. An image of the young Dark he'd had to kill to protect the little girl and her dog flashed in his head. He didn't regret saving the child or the animal. That didn't mean he liked taking the life of the one he had.

The lad might have been Dark, and he might have been torturing his little sister and the puppy, but the compulsion within Xaneth was meant for more. It was meant for the Others and their soldiers. Not everyday Dark.

Maybe it should be.

He shook his head to dislodge the voice inside. Xaneth didn't know what he was, but he knew for certain that he was no longer the Fae he'd once been. He never looked in mirrors for fear of what he would see.

Killing in anything but self-defense turned a Light. Were his eyes red now? Was there silver in his hair?

Did he even care?

Xaneth paused atop the latest building. He closed his eyes and contemplated his recent thoughts. Usaeil had stripped him of everything he'd been. She'd broken him down to his base self, thinking it would kill him.

It nearly did.

So many times.

Right now, the Reapers and Death wanted him as an ally. How much longer until they hunted *him*? That day would come. He was as certain of it as he was that he was now a monster. One with his old face, but still a monster.

There was a subtle shift in the air. Xaneth didn't need to look behind him to know that Aisling had caught up with him again. Or had he stayed so she would? He liked how she looked him in the eye as if she weren't afraid to see him. The *real* him. The Fae he'd kept buried century after century. Usaeil, the bitch, had let the real him loose during her torture. Too bad he hadn't been able to hunt his aunt down as he was doing with the Others.

Mercifully, Aisling didn't speak. Maybe it was dangerous for them both, but Xaneth got the impression that she accepted him. His thoughts were softening toward her, and he knew that was a treacherous path. Why should he care if a Reaper took it upon herself to follow him? She could be lying to get close so they could use him and then do away with him later.

It's what he would do.

Xaneth fought not to turn and look into her crimson eyes. He never should've intervened with her and the soldiers. She had been holding her own. She probably could've taken them out herself. But he hadn't been able to stop himself. At first, he'd simply watched her from the rooftop, mesmerized by her quick, fluid movements. She didn't take the routes he would have. Her mind saw things differently, and it allowed her to get the upper hand quickly.

But when the soldiers ganged up on her, Xaneth had seen red—literally. Before he knew it, he was in the alley taking his fury out on the Fae. It wasn't until he found himself about to touch Aisling's face that he'd left.

He'd been running from her ever since.

No. He'd been seeking evil. She played no part in his life. She might have wormed her way into his mind, but he had shoved her back out and slammed the door, bolting it so she could never get that close again.

Anger coiled within him. Anger at himself for being tempted by a pretty face and amazing battle skills. He had always been alone. He *would* always be alone. It was his destiny. Xaneth had fought against it for too long. It was time he accepted it. Embraced it.

Everyone else should, as well.

He opened his mouth to tell Aisling exactly that when he gagged as he caught a faint whiff of evil. He knew that scent well—the Others. They were still far away, but he would find them. Xaneth lifted his face and drew in as much of the smell as he could.

Then he began to hunt.

"For fek's sake," Aisling said with a roll of her eyes when Xaneth jumped away.

She'd gotten closer to Xaneth this time than she had before. Not including when he'd helped her in the alley. She had wanted to prove to him that she could be trusted. Given the stiffening of his body, he knew of her arrival. How could he see through her veil and know of her arrival? That wasn't possible for anyone but a Reaper —or Death and Cael—to do.

It had felt good to stand with him. She wanted to put a hand on his back to soothe some of the tension away, but he was like a wild animal. No one could get too close, or he'd bolt. She had to earn his trust. Otherwise, how could she help him?

Though she had no idea exactly how she *could* help him. He'd made it perfectly clear that he didn't want her near. Maybe she should take the hint. Then she was reminded of the powerful, overwhelming need to find Xaneth that had prompted her to look for him in the first place.

She put her hands on her hips and glared at the spot Xaneth had last been. Earlier, on the rooftop, he had looked her way. The agony in his eyes had knocked the breath from her. He battled not only physical pain but also emotional and mental trauma. The easy smile he'd once worn was gone, replaced by a face of granite that showed no gentleness or compassion.

It was the same look that stared back at her in the mirror when she dared to look.

Maybe that's why she felt such a need to seek him out. Aisling blew out a frustrated breath. She scanned the horizon, wondering where Xaneth had gone, when she recalled how he had lifted his head and sniffed the air like a dog taking in a scent.

"The Others," she murmured.

That's when she knew the Reapers were battling again. She had to be with her brethren now. Aisling grew still and quiet as she closed her eyes. It wouldn't take her long to find them. When she did, her eyes snapped open as she teleported to the castle.

Aisling strode into the monolithic structure with her arms held at her sides and her palms armed with orbs ready to throw. Cries of pain, bellows of fury, and the whoosh of magic being hurled filled the air. She followed the sounds, noting the piles of ash as she wound her way through the castle.

When she came to the open doors of the ballroom, she smiled and started running. She slid on her knees between Kyran and Neve and threw her orbs at the three soldiers they fought. Aisling ducked between the legs of another soldier as he screamed in pain. Then she put her foot flat and halted before jumping to her feet.

A soldier came at her from behind, reaching around to shove a sphere into her stomach. She threw back her head in reaction to the pain. The sound of bone crunching confirmed she had broken his nose. He loosened his arms enough for her to twist. Blood poured from his nose, and he reached for her. Aisling climbed over him until she was on his shoulders. With a twist, she leaned forward, taking them both to the ground. As they fell, she smashed two orbs against the sides of his head.

She ducked her head and rolled to her feet, dusting off the soldier's ash. There was no time to think about her wounds or the pain radiating through her. That would come later.

When she turned, she was shocked to see Ruarc veiled and fighting next to Balladyn. Obviously, a lot of shite had gone down that she wasn't aware of. A twinge struck her at not being with her family.

Then her gaze locked on Xaneth. He battled six soldiers on his own, though his gaze kept moving to a woman with a pixie cut and the first streaks of silver in her black hair. The way Xaneth moved was animalistic. The savagery on his face, the ferocity in his attack was impossible to turn away from.

Aisling realized that the soldiers weren't dying as easily as they should. These were different than the others. Aisling heard something behind her and turned to see a soldier rushing her. She waited until he was nearly upon her before jumping and tucking her body, flipping over him to land behind him. He whirled around. She saw the blade in time to lean back as it arced over her. The sword sliced the end of one of her braids that hung suspended in midair.

Aisling called her sword and straightened, plunging the blade into the soldier. To her shock, the tip of another sword pierced the soldier's chest. When he crumbled to ash, she found herself looking into Xaneth's eyes.

It was the second time he had come to her aid. He said nothing as he spun away, but Aisling wore a smile as she dodged an orb and turned to her next opponent.

"No!" a woman shouted.

Aisling glanced over to see a Light Fae staring at the same short-haired woman Xaneth had been glaring at. The woman held a man who had similar features to hers as white mist moved from him to the pixie-cut Fae.

"That's Lena, the leader of the Six," Eoghan told Aisling as he came even with her.

No wonder Xaneth had been in such a hurry to get here. Aisling was glad that she had joined her brethren for this battle. "Where are the other members?"

"This is about Lena." Eoghan was winded, his gaze locked on the woman.

The Light Fae female rushed Lena, but another woman grabbed hold of her and held her back.

Lena took a deep breath and smiled. "Who's next?"

"Enough, Lena," the Light being held stated.

Lena's red eyes slid to her. "You think you can stop me, Chevonne? Why don't you come and try?"

"Shite," Eoghan growled as he looked at Ruarc.

It was Xaneth who stepped forward. "Why don't you try me?"

Aisling moved forward to fight alongside Xaneth, but Eoghan held her in place. "Not yet."

How could she tell him that they couldn't let Xaneth die? If he did…she wasn't sure what would happen to her.

Lena raked her eyes over Xaneth. "I'd planned to get to the Reapers eventually. I might as well start now."

"I'm not a Reaper," Xaneth replied with a smile.

Something moved over Lena's face that looks suspiciously like alarm. It was gone so quickly, Aisling wasn't sure she had seen it at all. The room had grown eerily silent. The fighting halted as everyone watched Lena and Xaneth. Aisling noted that Xaneth had never looked so still and sure. Lena, on the other hand, wasn't as confident as before.

"If you run, I'll find you," Xaneth told her.

She smiled, but it was tight, forced. "I'm not going anywhere."

The moment the words were out, white mist began pouring from the chests of a group of Light Fae—all but Chevonne. It happened so quickly, no one had time to do anything.

Aisling started toward Lena, but a soldier blocked her way. She caught a glimpse of Xaneth as he sprinted to Lena, but she waved her hand and sent Xaneth through a stone wall. Aisling turned her attention to the battle and sent up a silent hope that Xaneth was all right.

She found herself beside Dubhan as they fought. The soldiers moved as quickly as they did. Worse, they seemed to have the same amount of power. Whatever advantage the Reapers usually had was gone.

"It's about time we're on equal footing," Dubhan said.

Aisling smiled in agreement. The Reapers weren't outnumbered. Soldiers had been killed, and more would follow. The Reapers, Erith, Cael, and Xaneth had done more damage than the soldiers ever could.

CHAPTER TWENTY-TWO

The heartache of seeing her father taken was nothing compared to watching her aunt kill the rest of her family in a split second. Chevonne fought between needing to scream, fight, and cry. But all she could do was stare at the neat piles of ash in shock and dismay.

She felt as if she looked down upon the entire event as if she were removed from her body. A whirlwind of emotions twisted and swirled around her, but thankfully, they couldn't touch her. She felt...heavy and numb. Like she was weighted down. It wouldn't last. Everything would pile on her with the force of a tsunami all too soon.

First, she had lost her beloved, Ruarc. That pain had seemed insurmountable. There was a gaping hole in her chest where her heart had been.

Then her father was killed. Her patient, devoted da. Now... everyone else. She couldn't turn to her mother for advice. Eileen and Shannon would no longer bother her with urgent texts or requests. Cillian wouldn't be there to make her laugh or help her out with a problem. She might not have been close to her uncle, but it was wrong for Lena to kill him in such a way.

Chevonne witnessing the eradication of her family had been

Lena's plan all along. Chevonne didn't know why she had been saved for last, and she didn't care. Whatever Lena intended had to be stopped. And there was only one group who could help her.

Chevonne looked at the closest Reaper to her. His red-ringed white eyes met hers. She didn't need to tell him what she wanted. He understood. Chevonne would die either way. It was better it be at the hands of a Reaper instead of her aunt or the Others.

At least she wouldn't feel all the hurt and loss of her family. She wouldn't feel anything soon. Would she find Ruarc in the afterlife? *Was* there an afterlife? It wasn't something they discussed. Why should beings that lived for thousands of years care what happened next? But now, she suddenly wanted to know. She needed to find Ruarc. To explain and apologize. She didn't care if they spent the rest of eternity floating through the cosmos, so long as they were together.

Chevonne steeled herself when she saw the white-haired Reaper shift slightly, an orb filling his hand. It probably wouldn't be painless, not after what she had done to Ruarc, but that was fine. Anything so her aunt didn't get her power.

The Reaper reared back his hand. As he released the magic, Chevonne heard someone shout. She could've sworn it was Ruarc. It had to be a figment of her imagination. Her brain putting something there that wasn't. Then, an arm came around her and yanked her to the side. Chevonne watched in panic as the magic sailed past her and into a soldier's throat.

"Did you really think you'd get away that easily?" Lena whispered in her ear.

Chevonne elbowed her aunt. She felt a moment of victory when she heard Lena grunt.

There was a commotion as the Fae Lena had thrown through the wall returned. His silver eyes glittered with fury as he stood among the dust and debris. He stepped over the crumbling stones and rushed Lena. Chevonne closed her eyes. If the Reaper couldn't kill her, maybe whoever this was could.

∼

One minute, Lena and Chevonne were there. The next, they weren't. Neither was the man who had attacked them. Ruarc released a bellow and turned his wrath on the soldiers who remained. There was no way he would let any of them leave now that it had been revealed they had some of the Reapers' magic.

He wasn't the only one. The rest of the Reapers attacked, but Erith left the most carnage. Ruarc was furious when no more soldiers remained. He turned in a slow circle, searching for another foe.

"Aisling," Rordan said with a smile.

Ruarc stared at the female Reaper, who stood unblinking. She finally pulled her gaze away and look at Erith. "Where's Xaneth?"

"And Chevonne?" Ruarc added.

Kyran wiped away blood and sweat from his face. "Lena's power more than quadrupled. We need to find them immediately."

"We all saw it," Eoghan said. "We know what's at stake."

Aisling shook her head of black and silver braids. "She put Xaneth through a wall."

"I don't want to think about what she could do to us now," Cathal said.

Ruarc didn't want to talk. He wanted to fight. He focused on where Lena and Chevonne had been. Did Lena teleport them away? Or had it been Xaneth? Where would they go?

"She intends to take Chevonne's magic," Balladyn said as he walked up.

Ruarc glanced at him and nodded. "Why didn't she do it with the others?"

"Something I've been wondering," Cael chimed in.

Bradach blew out a breath. "We all have."

"Something was up between Lena and Xaneth," Aisling said. "She's warier of him than us."

Erith met Cael's gaze. "I noticed that."

"I did, as well," Fintan replied.

Neve threw up her hands in frustration. "That's all great and everything, but we need to find them first and ask questions later. Doesn't Chevonne still have the tracker?"

"I always said you were the smart one," Kyran told her as he smirked at Talin.

Talin rolled his eyes. "You vex me."

Ruarc tuned them out. He focused on Chevonne. He was a new Reaper who had yet to discover all the things his new power gave him. But right now, all he wanted was to find his woman. He kicked himself for not getting to her before Lena. Time wasn't on their side. If he didn't find Chevonne... He couldn't finish the thought.

"We have one shot," Rordan said as he came up on Ruarc's other side.

Balladyn cracked his neck. "Then let's do this."

Death moved to stand in front of Ruarc. She held his gaze. She didn't speak. Instead, she gave a single nod and lifted her sword overhead. The room swam with Erith's magic, churning and whipping ferociously. Cael and Eoghan released their magic, and the rest of the Reapers followed. Ruarc had never felt anything like it before. It was both terrifying and thrilling. It was no wonder the Others wanted the Reapers gone. But it once more showed Ruarc that if Erith and the Reapers really wanted to take over, they could.

Anticipation rushed through him, his heart beating faster. They would find Lena and Chevonne. He fisted his hands as he imagined how he would take out his fury on Lena for harming Chevonne and taking her family from her.

The moment Erith teleported, Ruarc followed. They appeared in a manicured lawn with the stars winking from above. Sea salt was heavy in the air. He didn't recognize the location. There was a chance that Lena had taken Chevonne to an Other stronghold, but since Lena wanted all the power, he wasn't sure she would chance that.

Erith glanced at Cael and Eoghan. The two spread out and motioned to the rest of the Reapers. Ruarc followed Eoghan's orders to go to the right. He moved through hedges and past beds of roses. The night was eerily still, the silence almost warning them of the malevolent force ahead.

A shout of fury split the night, stopping them in their tracks. It had come from ahead of them through the grove of trees. None of the Reapers made a sound, but a ripple of awareness ran through them. A male had bellowed. Ruarc needed to move faster so he could reach Chevonne and find out if she was unharmed.

Cael and Eoghan directed them to encircle the grove. Ruarc wished he could see through the trees. He just needed a glimpse of Chevonne. To see her alive. That was all he needed to calm his nerves.

The Reapers entered the woods. Balladyn was to Ruarc's right and Bradach to his left. Ruarc had no idea where Erith was, but he knew she was near. They moved cautiously, quietly, but with purpose. Their gazes trained on the center of the clearing and their quarry. Each step took them closer to finding Lena, Xaneth, and Chevonne.

A grunt of pain sounded, followed by the creak of a tree as something slammed into it. A noise that sounded like a snarl filled the air, followed by a distinctive feminine wheeze.

"You will die tonight."

Ruarc frowned at Xaneth's words. Who was this Fae?

Lena's laugh bounced through the grove. "Wishful thinking."

"I got you here, didn't I?" Xaneth retorted.

"You got lucky."

"Luck has nothing to do with this."

Ruarc was close enough now to see Xaneth and Lena circling each other. Trees around them had been blackened by magic, while some smaller trees had been completely destroyed. Both Xaneth and Lena bore injuries, proving that Xaneth had held his own against the Other leader.

Ruarc searched the area for Chevonne and found her lying unconscious on the ground. He wanted to run to her, but she was too far away. He glanced at Balladyn to see his veil raised. Ruarc noticed that the Reapers all had theirs up. He had never lowered his.

To Ruarc's surprise, Xaneth glanced away from Lena toward Aisling. Ruarc frowned. Could Xaneth see them? Only Reapers, Death, and Cael could see another Reaper while veiled. But it was obvious that Xaneth saw them. Odd that he had looked at Aisling first, but that wasn't Ruarc's concern.

"Enough of this," Xaneth murmured.

In the next instant, he pummeled Lena with magic. Only she expected it and blocked the orbs before sending her magic toward him. Xaneth was thrown back into a tree. A loud crack rent the air, something that could've been the tree or Xaneth's spine.

Movement caught Ruarc's eye. His heart jumped into his throat when he saw Chevonne stir.

CHAPTER TWENTY-THREE

Chevonne pushed through the fog of oblivion. Urgency propelled her awake. With consciousness came the aches in her body—and her heart. The moment she roused, an image surfaced of Ruarc dying quickly followed that of her father and the rest of her family.

No longer was she removed from her emotions. They swallowed her, consuming her so completely that she knew she would never surface. Her grief drowned her. But she had to tread water enough to end her aunt. Both seemed like impossibilities. But if she didn't, who would?

She heard a groan of pain. Her eyes cracked open. The dark scene before her was blurry and distorted. She could just make out two figures engaged in battle. Her heart leapt when she locked eyes with the male. Was that...could that be Ruarc?

Chevonne blinked rapidly and pushed up on an elbow. The hope died a swift, agonizing death when she realized that it was the same man she'd thought might kill her. Tears blurred her vision. She hastily swallowed her pain and reached for the anger. Rage would fuel her. It would give her the strength to do what was necessary.

She locked gazes with Lena. Her aunt was hurt. That made Chevonne smile. She wanted Lena to scream in pain, to writhe in agony. Just as Chevonne was. That was the only thing that might reconcile the ache within.

Chevonne's legs were unsteady as she got to her feet. Her head throbbed, but she pushed it aside. Lena was engrossed with the battle, giving Chevonne the opportunity she needed. She called the dagger her mother had gifted her with and gripped the pommel tightly. Chevonne bided her time patiently. Fortunately, she didn't have long to wait. Lena stumbled backward—right to her. Chevonne lifted her arm with the dagger's blade pointing down to drive into her aunt's heart.

Lena's head snapped to her, and she held out her hand. Chevonne's body halted. She tried to move and continue the dagger's downward trajectory, but her muscles wouldn't respond. Then she felt as if she were being pulled apart in a million different directions.

Ruarc was done waiting. He couldn't sit by and let Lena take Chevonne's life and magic. He leapt from his position and tried to cut through whatever Lena did to hold Chevonne, but his magic did nothing. The white mist moved quicker and quicker from Chevonne. Her eyes were wide, fear clouding them.

"Nooo!" he bellowed and struck Lena with his magic.

He blasted her again and again without seeing any effect. Ruarc wouldn't give up, though. He gritted his teeth and continued.

He had no idea when his brethren joined him. Erith's battle cry as she used her blade to sever the link Lena had with Chevonne alerted him. Ruarc watched in horror as Chevonne tumbled to the ground. Fury surged through him as he formed an orb and drew back his hand to hurl it at Lena.

Lena threw out her hands. The magic that rippled over them wiped away their veils. Ruarc lobbed more magic. Lena's gaze landed on him as she blocked the orb. Her nostrils flared as her gaze narrowed in disbelief.

"No," she murmured.

Every Reaper had magic at the ready to throw her way. Death stalked toward Lena with her black sword in hand.

Lena sneered. "I'm not afraid of you."

"That's your first mistake," Erith replied.

Suddenly, the Light was between the two women. He took a blow of magic from Lena on his shoulder.

"Xaneth! Get out of the way," Death demanded.

He ignored her and took a step toward Lena. Ruarc was done chasing the Others. He was finished letting the Six run things. He threw his orb and watched Lena jerk to the side at the impact.

The other Reapers pummeled her, as well. Lena tried to block the onslaught, but there were too many. She dropped to her knees. Ruarc smiled. They were going to win. Chevonne and her family would be avenged. He wanted to shout for joy.

Chevonne sucked in a breath, her lungs expanding. So, that's what dying felt like. It sucked. She didn't want to do that again.

The sound of someone shouting had her lifting her head. She stood in amazement, looking at the Reapers who battered her aunt with magic. Lena was losing, badly. Chevonne realized that her dagger was still in her hand. She jumped to her feet and rushed through the Reapers. Lena's eyes widened at the sight of her.

Her aunt whispered something that made Xaneth grab his head and double over. Then she teleported away. Chevonne reached her aunt and jerked up her hand just as her aunt teleported. Chevonne bellowed her anger, uncaring about the orbs falling around her, missing her by centimeters.

The force of her attack sent her tumbling to the ground. She climbed to her feet and stared furiously at the place Lena had been, huddled over as her breath filled the silence. There, on the ground, was a portion of her aunt's ear. At least her blade had found its mark.

Chevonne turned her head to Xaneth, who writhed on the ground for a moment until he went limp. That's when she realized that she stood in the middle of a group of Reapers. She lifted her gaze and looked at each one, slowly turning as she did. She did a double-take when her eyes landed on Ruarc.

A cry of surprise and hope bubbled from her lips as tears welled in her eyes. "Ruarc?"

"It's me."

He looked different somehow. She wanted to run to him, to touch his face and hold him close. "I...I thought you died."

His gaze briefly lowered. "I did."

Chevonne was acutely aware that they weren't alone. She swallowed nervously, moving her dagger from one hand to the other. "I'm sorry. For all of it. Lena threatened my family and you."

"I know." He spoke without ire. "None of it was your fault."

She searched his face to see if he was lying, but the truth of what he said was in his pale silver eyes. She'd thought him being dead was the worst thing she'd have to bear. But now, she would have to live the rest of her life knowing that he was alive and not with her.

The silence between them stretched. She had much she wanted to say, but she couldn't get the words out.

"We had her," Torin stated.

Eoghan shook his head angrily. "We may not get that close again."

"Because Xaneth got in the way," Ruarc said as he pointed at the Fae.

A Dark female with long, black and silver braids and red eyes moved between Ruarc and Xaneth. "We may be family now, but I *will* kick your ass," she stated, fire in her crimson eyes.

"Lena would be dead now had he not interfered," Ruarc replied.

Chevonne was thankful that everyone's attention was on someone else. She glanced at Xaneth. She had no idea who he was, but she wanted to know. Her aunt was scared of him in a way that she wasn't frightened of the Reapers or Death.

"We need to take Xaneth somewhere safe," the Dark female said. "Somewhere he can't get away."

The woman with lavender eyes shook her head. "I'm not holding him prisoner, Aisling."

To Chevonne's shock, Xaneth's eyes opened. He looked right at her before disappearing. Her gaze jerked to Ruarc to find him watching her.

"Fek," Aisling ground out.

For a long, awkward moment, no one spoke. Chevonne thought about leaving, but where would she go? Who would she run to? Her family was gone. She closed her eyes as the events of the day piled onto her. She didn't want to break down in front of the group, but she wasn't sure how much longer she could keep it together.

Then, arms she knew well wrapped around her as Ruarc pulled her against him. "You don't have to hold it in any longer," he whispered.

She didn't want to give in to the yawning void of sorrow and despair. She might never pull herself out of it. Yet, cradled in the comfortable arms of the man she loved, Chevonne's resolve buckled. She clung to him as the first sob burst free.

Ruarc's heart broke for Chevonne. She had stood resiliently against her aunt. With the battle finished, there was nothing more for Chevonne to focus on. Ruarc had seen her about to crumble beneath the weight of her grief. He didn't know or care if he was allowed to hold Chevonne.

When he went to her, the Reapers and Cael left. Erith remained. She gave him a nod, sadness in her gaze before she too departed.

The instant Ruarc's arms were around Chevonne, he felt as if he had come home. He closed his eyes against her warmth and softness. He loved her more than anything. He didn't know how he would survive without her. Maybe he didn't have to. Most Reapers had mates. Why couldn't he? There had to be a way that he and Chevonne could be together. Whatever it was, he would do it. Whatever boon Death required, whatever service she deemed worthy, he would undertake it.

Chevonne cried, her shoulders shaking with her sobs. He wished he could take away her pain, or at the very least remove the memory of witnessing her family members' deaths. He might be a Reaper with great power, but he didn't think his magic could do that.

He didn't know how long they stood there before he realized that her tears had stopped. It felt good to hold her. He never wanted to let her go.

"I'm so sorry for what I did to you," she said with a sniff.

He rubbed his hands up and down her back. "You don't have to apologize. You did what you had to do for your family. I did the same."

"I'm the reason Lena...that she..."

"No," he stated firmly. "That's on her. Not you."

Chevonne was silent for a moment. "Are you a Reaper?"

"Yes."

She sniffed again and lifted her head from his chest. Her eyes were bloodshot, and her lashes spiked from her tears. "What happens now?"

"I don't know."

"Is there a way we can be together? After I earn your trust, that is."

He smiled as he wiped at the tear tracks on her cheeks. "You still have my trust. I love you. I always have. And I always will."

Fresh tears spilled from her eyes. "I never stopped loving you. Even when we couldn't be together, I loved you. I love you now and will always."

Ruarc closed his eyes as he pulled her close. He tangled his fingers in her hair. "Is there somewhere safe you can go? Somewhere Lena can't find you?"

"Yes," Chevonne answered after a pause.

The last thing Ruarc wanted to do was let her go. Lena was still out there, and he knew she wouldn't give up trying to take Chevonne's magic. But he had to speak to Erith. He needed to know if he and Chevonne could be together. Erith had told him that he had to give up his old life and everyone in it. No doubt she'd meant Chevonne, as well.

But other Reapers were mated. Why couldn't he have that?

"Go there and stay until I call for you." He pulled back so he could see her. Ruarc cupped her face and lowered his lips to hers. "Please."

She tried to smile, but she didn't quite make it. He knew she thought he was letting her go for good. Ruarc didn't want to give her false hope. It was better he keep what he was doing to himself until he had answers from Erith.

"Be safe," Chevonne whispered.

Ruarc forced himself to release her. The instant he did, she vanished. He drew in a shaky breath and raked a hand through his hair. Fuck. How had his life gotten so complicated? He didn't regret taking Death's offer, but he never expected to be in the position he was now.

He blew out a breath and squeezed his eyes closed. What did he say to Erith? How did he even begin to tell her how much he loved and needed Chevonne?

"It might be easier if you speak."

Ruarc's eyes snapped open. He turned to find Erith behind him. She had changed out of her battle clothes into another black ensemble. This one a wispy black dress of gauze that hung in soft layers on her petite frame. Her long, blue-black hair was parted on the side and draped loosely about her shoulders.

"I'm not blind," Erith continued. "I know what you want."

He swallowed, hope and fear churning in his gut. "I love her."

"And she loves you."

Ruarc licked his lips. "I know I'm new to the Reapers. I don't know all the rules or how to do things, but I do know many Reapers have mates."

"They do," she replied evenly.

"I'll do anything you ask of me—anything—if Chevonne and I can be together." He swallowed and added, "Please."

Erith studied him for a long minute. "Do you think me so cruel that I would torment you more?"

"I don't know you well, but from what I've seen, you've been fair and gracious."

"It's true that, at one time, the Reapers weren't allowed to have relationships. That rule destroyed my first group and made an enemy that nearly cost me everything. I might keep the balance between good and evil, but I can't prevent love. When I stopped trying is when I discovered what an amazing family I had. Everyone with a Reaper has earned their way into our family."

Ruarc thought about Chevonne's betrayal and inwardly cringed. "Chevonne had no choice. Lena put her in a no-win position."

"I know," Erith said with a smile. "I'm glad you came to see that. She did earn her way."

He grinned as he thought of Chevonne. "I love her. I know she would never willingly hurt me."

"What about what Lena did to you?"

Ruarc thought about that for a moment before he shrugged. "This is where I'm supposed to be. This," he said, motioning between them, "is what I'm supposed to do. I want revenge, but not because Lena killed me. I want it for what she's done to Chevonne and everyone else."

Erith nodded. "Good. Go get Chevonne and bring her home. Just make sure you aren't followed. Lena will be searching for her. The only way to keep Chevonne out of her aunt's hands is to get Chevonne off this realm."

Ruarc couldn't contain his smile.

CHAPTER TWENTY-FOUR

Ruarc had told her to go somewhere safe. She didn't have anywhere to go, so she went to the cottage. She wrapped her arms around herself and turned in a circle to look at everything. Ruarc had changed very little from the last time she had been here.

This had been their special place. It was the perfect spot for her to feel close to Ruarc. Especially since she wasn't sure if she would see him again or not. The only thing that kept her going was Ruarc. His strong shoulders had taken her grief and tears, making the load she carried a little lighter.

Chevonne walked to the bedroom. She thought of the recording under the bed at Ruarc's penthouse. She wanted it, but she wasn't sure about returning there. Maybe later. She walked to his bed and curled up on it, hugging his pillow against her. She tried not to think about her parents, sisters, uncle, or cousin, but it was impossible. Lena had taken them without hesitation.

Chevonne thought about all the times she had sat at a table to eat with her aunt. It turned her stomach that she had been that close to evil and never knew it. How could she not have seen it? How could any of them have missed it?

It did no good to think about that. The past was the past. There was no changing it. The future, however, was another matter. So was the present. Lena would come for her again. Chevonne tried to think of where she could go so her aunt couldn't find her—or send someone to get her.

She was racking her brain on where to go when she heard Ruarc call her name. Happiness shot through her, dispelling all her dark thoughts. She jumped up and immediately went to him. To her shock, he was still in the grove.

"Hi," he said with a smile.

She worried at how happy he was as she returned his grin. "Hi."

"Do you want to be with me?"

"You know I do."

"I'm not free to do as I want," he cautioned. "I follow Death's commands. There will be things I do, places I go, that you can't follow. You wouldn't be alone, though. There are other mates there."

Her brows shot up on her forehead. "There are?"

"Yes," he said with a chuckle. "You've been through a lot today. If you need time—"

"I need you," she said as she threw her arms around him. "I've only always needed you."

His arms tightened around her. "You've always had me."

"Can we really be together?"

He leaned back and nodded as he looked into her eyes. "Absolutely."

"Can it start right now? We don't have to wait, do we?"

Ruarc laughed and said between kisses, "No waiting."

Chevonne sank into his kiss. Her world had been upended, but Ruarc's love would help her mend. He grabbed her hips and rocked his arousal against her. She ground against him, needing him inside her.

"Wait," he said breathlessly.

She opened her eyes to find herself on an isle in the middle of a large body of water. "Where are we?"

"About to step across to your new home," he said and took her hand.

Chevonne followed him through a Fae doorway. Her mouth fell open as she gazed at the beauty around her. The burst of color from all the flowers was nearly blinding. The birds' chirps, the buzzing of bees, and the soft flutter of a dragonfly's wings descended a calm upon her that she had never felt before.

She stopped to sniff several blossoms as Ruarc led her through the flowers. She sighed when a breeze ruffled her hair and made the leaves of the trees rustle. Then she saw the white tower.

"Death's residence," Ruarc explained. "This is her realm. Hers and her Reapers'. As well as their mates."

Chevonne jerked her head to him. "You mean…?"

"Yes," he said with a laugh. "Lena will never find you here."

Chevonne was speechless. "I know this isn't just about me. If Lena can't get to me, she can't get my magic, and therefore can't become as powerful as she wants. I'm grateful that I have a place to feel safe."

"Me, too," he said and squeezed her hand. "I've not met all the mates yet. We'll do that together. For now, Death informed me that we can live anywhere we want. Simply pick a place."

She turned to him and cupped his arousal. "Find a place. Quick."

"We don't need a house for that," he said with a wink.

Chevonne laughed as Ruarc teleported them to an island with turquoise waters and palm trees swaying.

"Will this do?" he asked before kissing her.

She tried to answer but forgot the question when his tongue swept into her mouth. Then nothing mattered as they ripped each other's clothes off, seeking the passion and love they knew awaited them.

EPILOGUE

Two weeks later…

Erith watched Ruarc and Chevonne. The newest couple to their family fit in well. Chevonne's gratitude showed in everything she did. She had come to Erith and thanked her profusely, as well as professed her loyalty to the Reapers.

As for Ruarc, he was a natural-born Reaper. Erith hated how each of the Reapers had been hurt, but those she picked were the best of the best. They proved time and again that they were up for any battle, any foe. They had never let her down.

It was up to her not to let them down now.

She was still worried about the Six, especially Lena. It was bad enough that Lena had stolen as much magic as she had. Erith admonished herself for not knowing the Quinlans were once the Muldowneys.

"You're doing it again."

Erith looked at Cael. His purple gaze held hers. Erith cleared her throat, remembering that their large family was having dinner together. "What am I doing?"

"Frowning because you're thinking about the Others, most especially Lena."

He knew her so well. She gave him a side-eye and smiled. "I don't know what you're talking about."

"We'll get them."

Her smile faded as she heard the seriousness of his words. She turned her head to him. "We have to."

"Should we talk to the Dragon Kings? Alert them about what's going on?"

"Con and Rhi are still on Zora."

"Maybe you should check on them."

She shook her head. "If things get too bad, I'll alert the Kings."

Cael blew out a breath. "I'm not saying we need them."

"The truth is we might. I felt Lena's magic growing. It's significant, babe."

"She didn't get Chevonne's."

Erith rolled her eyes. "I can't imagine where we'd be if she had."

"We'd be right here. You would've unleashed Hell upon her."

He said it with a smile, but Erith didn't return it. "I'm worried about the power the Six are gaining. Learning that Lena took magic from the Reapers during battle and gave it to her soldiers infuriates me."

"She's crafty, I'll give her that," Cael said. "You're Death. You command a group of powerful Fae. We will win. We've figured it out in the past. We will this time, too." He wrapped his arms around her and kissed her softly.

Erith rested her head on his shoulder and listened to a story Chevonne told of Ruarc's youth that had everyone laughing. Cael was right. Erith would unleash Hell. Because no one threatened her family.

～

Isle of Skye

"Well?"

Rhona looked around at the Druids gathered about her. People she had known her entire life. She trained with them. Knew them personally. Yet, they weren't acting like those she knew. "Did none of you hear what I said about the Fae Others and the Reapers?"

"Those Others are after the Reapers," a Druid said. "We aren't. We've not given the Reapers cause to look our way. They even asked for our help."

Rhona reached for the last of her patience. "The Dragon Kings eradicated the original Others. They will come for us if we do this. So will the Reapers."

"The Druids in Ireland already have a group," another Druid replied. "Do this, or we'll find another to lead."

Rhona narrowed her eyes. "Corann appointed me as your leader for a reason."

"Then act like it."

～

Thank you for reading **DARK ALPHA'S PASSION**! I hope you loved Ruarc and Chevonne's story as much as I loved writing it. Next up in the Dark World is the Dragon Kings book, DRAGON ETERNAL.

The seduction begins.

Buy DRAGON ETERNAL now at
https://dgrant.co/3w1EgIB

～

To find out when new books release
SIGN UP FOR MY NEWSLETTER today at
http://www.tinyurl.com/DonnaGrantNews.

Join my Facebook group, Donna Grant Groupies, for exclusive
giveaways and sneak peeks of future books.

If you love the Reaper series, you'll be thrilled to read a fan
favorite's story in book 15, DARK ALPHA'S COMMAND...

When love is a battlefield, the heart takes no prisoners.

Buy DARK ALPHA'S COMMAND today at
https://dgrant.co/3JebuKp

~

Keep reading for a excerpt from DRAGON ETERNAL and a
special sneak peek at DARK ALPHA'S COMMAND...

EXCERPT OF DRAGON ETERNAL

DRAGON KINGS SERIES®, BOOK 4

In the next installment of her captivating new Dragon Kings® series, *New York Times* bestselling author Donna Grant® connects an enigmatic and determined Dragon King and a courtesan sent to tempt him to his doom.

He's a man of few words, but she fills his soul with poetry.

Quiet. Brooding. Capable. Shaw's mission is simple: Root out Stonemore's leader and determine what the Divine has in store for the people of Zora and the Kings. Just as he gets started, however, a breathtakingly beautiful woman finds and tempts him like no other. Nothing can stop him from engaging in the pleasures she offers. After all, pillow talk is sometimes the best way to uncover secrets.

Nia's life has never been hers. From starving on the streets to becoming a slave to the Divine, she merely does what's needed to survive. But when her latest assignment brings her face-to-face with a handsome man who makes her feel things she's never experienced before, she begins to see that while she's been living, she's not really thriving.

As truths are revealed, and Nia's blinders are removed, she realizes that she can no longer sit by and allow things to continue as they have been in her city. It's time to take a stand. With Shaw by her side, they spark a war so many have tried to avoid. But the injustices being perpetrated must be stopped—no matter the cost.

Chapter One

Cairnkeep

Shaw stood with his eyes closed on the cliff near Cairnkeep and listened to the dragons. The flaps of their wings, their roars as they called to one another, and the whoosh as they flew. He had missed the sounds the most.

He drew in a deep breath and slowly released it, enjoying the feel of the sun upon his face. The dragons' peaceful noises calmed the rage inside him. Most of his Dragon King brethren pretended that fury didn't exist. But it was there.

Always.

Until now. For the first time in ages, he felt as if things were back to normal.

Except, they weren't.

They were far from it, actually. Yet, for this moment, he could pretend as if they were on Earth, that the dragons had never been sent away, and that they had never heard of humans.

Sadly, all of that was simply wishing. Because the mortals had come, there had been a war, and the dragons *had* been sent away. For so long, Shaw, like many Dragon Kings, had feared they would never find their dragons again.

He opened his eyes and looked at the mountains around him. Zora. A realm the Dragon Kings only recently discovered that had been the dragons' home since that fateful day on Earth. Zora was a spectacular realm. Majestic mountains, breathtaking plains, stunning forests, and everything in between. Every vista was dazzling in its splendor. The sky was brighter, the oceans bluer, the grass greener.

Shaw felt whole once more. And it was all because he was with the dragons.

Yet he knew his time on Zora was limited. He and the other Dragon Kings were there simply to seek out something that had been able to attack and killed dragons—something that had never happened before.

The crunch of grass alerted him that someone approached. He glanced over to find Merrill. Shaw had never been much of a talker. Merrill made up for that since he never seemed to shut up. He wondered if Merrill would give one of his pep talks. The thought nearly made Shaw smile, but he swallowed it before Merrill could see.

"I'll never get tired of this view. Or *any* view with dragons," Merrill said. "I saw all of you every day. I suppose that should be enough, but it wasna."

Shaw grunted. The Kings had hidden their identities from the humans on Earth, only taking flight at night or during storms.

"I missed seeing my Oranges. I missed gazing at my clan," Merrill continued, his dark blue eyes on the dragons in the distance.

Shaw glanced at him. The pain etched on Merrill's face was the same every Dragon King endured from the instant they'd sent their dragons away to save them. But this was the first time in ages that he had seen it on Merrill's face. Shaw frowned, a small niggle of worry taking root. Then he realized who he was thinking about.

If anyone had gotten past the anger, heartbreak, and misery, it was Merrill. He had been born blessed with a sunny outlook. There were times that Shaw had been jealous of Merrill's ability, but Shaw had accepted who he was long ago.

Merrill pulled his gaze from the dragons and shuttered his

agony. "I wonder if they're changing up our patrol area. The desert area I had was pretty, but I'd love to see some water. Maybe look for some caves."

Shaw shrugged. He had no idea why he and Merrill had all been called back to Cairnkeep. For weeks, each of the Kings had had a designated area along the dragon border in hopes of finding the new threat. It was bad enough that this new invisible foe had killed dragons, but the twin rulers of Zora—Brandr and Eurwen—had also been attacked.

"I think this has something to do with Cullen."

Shaw frowned at Merrill.

Merrill ran a hand through his dirty blond hair and jerked his thumb over his shoulder. "Cullen arrived a few minutes ago. I was hoping he'd bring his mate, Tamlyn, with him. I can no' wait to meet a Banshee."

Shaw turned to face Cairnkeep. The twins hadn't built a large castle or any such structure. They had kept things simple with separate cottages to call their own. Shaw didn't blame them. He wouldn't have built anything if it were him. Then again, the twins were half-dragon, half-Fae.

And were incredibly powerful as children of the King of Dragon Kings—Constantine—and a royal Light Fae—Rhi. The twins had seen the mistakes the Kings had made on Earth, and they had been determined to do better when humans began arriving on Zora.

Shaw had to admit that Brandr and Eurwen had done things well. They had sectioned off a good-sized area for the mortals and told them to do with it what they wanted, but that they wouldn't get more land. So far, the humans hadn't tried. They would. Eventually. Shaw was curious to see what the twins would do when that time came. Hopefully, he and the other Kings would still have access to Zora to find out.

"I wonder how long we'll be allowed to stay after we find this new enemy," Merrill said.

Shaw shook his head and shrugged.

"It's easy for them to look at our decisions and point out where

we went wrong, but we did the best we could," Merrill continued.
"It also seems like the twins' relationship with Con and Rhi is
improving. I think that's a move in the right direction."

Shaw shot him a dry look. Merrill was crazy if he thought
millennia of contention between parents and children could be
healed in a few months. Granted, Con and Rhi hadn't even realized
they *had* children. That was because Erith, also known as Death,
had intervened to save Rhi after she was attacked. By taking the
embryos so Rhi could heal, Erith had created a ripple through time
that had affected everyone. Rhi hadn't known that she was
pregnant, and once she was healed, Erith hadn't been able to put
the babies back.

So, the twins had a healthy dose of anger toward their parents.
Like Merrill had said, it was easy for someone, especially a child, to
look back and point out the mistakes of a person's past. Con was far
from perfect, but he had set aside his wants and needs—and his love
for Rhi—for the Dragon Kings.

Fortunately, Rhi and Con had found their way back to each
other—as all of them had known they would. Now, the couple was
getting to know their children.

"Here they come," Merrill said.

Shaw spotted the dragons flying toward them. He caught sight
of Con's gold scales as well as Cullen's garnet ones. It wasn't long
before he spotted Vaughn's teal scales, and beside him, Eurwen's
peach body and gold wings. The last one to arrive was Brandr. His
gold scales faded to beige on his stomach.

Shaw walked alongside Merrill toward the others as Cullen
joined them. Dragons had always been solid colors on Earth
because they'd kept to their clans. They hadn't stayed in those clans
after finding Zora. They intermingled, which Shaw liked. That
meant that Brandr and Eurwen weren't the only dual-toned dragons
now, though their coloring came from the fact that they were
half-Fae.

"Thank you for coming so quickly," Eurwen said as she smiled
first at Merrill and then at Shaw. She had Rhi's silver eyes and Con's

blond hair. Her fair coloring set her apart from her twin with his black eyes and black hair.

Brandr crossed his arms over his chest and widened his stance. "We realize that you two were asked to come to Zora to help us search for our new enemy, but there has been a development."

Shaw's gaze moved to Cullen.

"What might that be?" Merrill asked.

Cullen blew out a breath before his pale brown eyes looked between the two of them. "In my region, I saved a woman and a young lad. That woman, Tamlyn, is my mate."

"We heard," Merrill replied.

Shaw nodded when Cullen looked at him.

"What you might no' have heard yet is that Tamlyn's Banshee ability allows her to save children with magic from being killed." Cullen glanced behind him, his gaze focused in the distance as if he couldn't wait to get back to his mate. "The city, Stonemore, has a law that states that anyone with magic is to be killed. When they discover children with magic, they take them to the priests and then execute them."

Merrill looked aghast. "Bloody hell. Bairns? Who would do that?"

Fury ripped through Shaw. Just one more reason to loathe mortals.

And another reason for why he and the other Kings should have wiped them out when they had the chance.

"They do that so they doona have to fight adults later, those who have the audacity to stand against them," Con replied.

Shaw realized what the group wanted of him and Merrill. "You want us to go into the city and find these bastards."

"Yes, and no," Vaughn said.

Rhi suddenly appeared. All Fae could teleport. Even the twins were able to do it for short distances. Rhi pulled her long, black hair away from her face and put it in a ponytail. "Everything is fine with Tamlyn and the others."

Relief filled Cullen's face. Shaw watched him curiously. There was no doubt in his mind that love existed. Too many of his brethren had found their mates to say otherwise. Yet some were meant to love. And some weren't.

He was in the latter camp. Shaw became a Dragon King to keep his clan safe and rule justly. Once the dragons left, his purpose had shifted to ensuring that the Kings survived and remained together. And he couldn't do that if he was weak—and falling in love would make him vulnerable.

A muscle worked in Brandr's jaw. "Cullen is known in Stonemore now. In order to save Tamlyn and a group of kids, he shifted and gained the attention of everyone in the city. No' a smart move."

"What kind of Dragon King would I be if I'd allowed them to die, simply to stay hidden?" Cullen demanded, his anger palpable.

"Suffice it to say that everyone is on high alert," Rhi added.

Merrill ran a hand over his jaw. "What is it you want us to do?"

"Infiltrate the city," Eurwen continued. "Separately. Have no contact with each other that anyone can see. They'll be searching for magic, which means you'll have to make sure not to use any that anyone might see."

Cullen nodded in agreement. "You should be able to communicate using our telepathic link. The only time I wasna able to do so was when our new foe was close by."

"They were there?" Shaw asked, suddenly anxious to get to Stonemore.

Cullen's nostrils flared. "You can no' see them. No' straight on. Out of the corner of your eye, it's almost like seeing a wave in the air. A shimmer. That's it, or them, or whatever or whoever the bloody hell it is. It took me down in dragon form. Be warned, when struck with its magic, I couldna move."

"Whatever magic they use freezes you," Eurwen added. She stepped closer to her mate, Vaughn.

Brandr dropped his arms to his sides. "I've never encountered anything like it before. I didna see it coming."

"None of us did," Cullen said.

Shaw filed that information away.

"What's our objective?" Merrill asked.

Cullen snorted, a muscle jumping in his jaw. "If it were up to me, I'd tell you to kill any priests you come across. Then find the Divine, whoever the bastard is that's ruling Stonemore, and put an end to them. Immediately."

"But it isna up to you," Brandr snapped. He glared at Cullen.

Eurwen lifted her chin. "We need more information on the city. Its inhabitants, who the Divine is, the priests, who might help free the children. Anything and everything. The more you can get, the better."

In other words, they were spies. Shaw could think of a million different ways to use a Dragon King—including what Cullen wanted—but that would have to wait for another day. For now, he would get all the intel they wanted.

"The sooner we get there, the sooner we find what's needed," Merrill said.

Con stepped forward. "Make sure we doona start a war."

"Seems like that has already happened, starting with the killing of children," Merrill added, a spark of anger in his eyes.

Con shrugged. "Be that as it may, this isna our realm. We're guests. Eurwen and Brandr are in charge."

Shaw had only ever taken orders from Con. He almost asked what Con would do if he were in charge, but that probably wasn't the best question to pose at the moment.

"Watch yourselves. Doona underestimate the mortals at Stonemore," Cullen cautioned.

∼

Buy DRAGON ETERNAL now at
https://dgrant.co/3w1EgIB

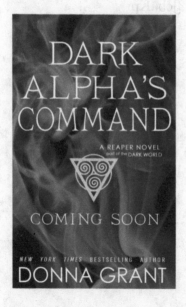

From *New York Times* bestselling author Donna Grant® comes another action-packed installment in her thrilling Reaper series, featuring a brotherhood of elite assassins who wage war on the Fae at Death's behest—and the women who dare to love them.

There is no escaping a Reaper. I am an elite assassin, part of a brotherhood that only answers to Death. And when Death says your time is up, I'm coming for you...

I've been a part of so many different worlds I'm not sure who I am or where I fit in anymore. Honestly, with everything I've been through, being called across realms and encountering the beautiful

Druid who instantly captures my attention—and my heart—shouldn't have surprised me. But it did. Not as much as discovering how it feels to brush against her magic, however. Now, we must navigate these new waters and fight against our latest threat, hoping that our combined power and that of our allies is enough to defeat our foe. Because the Fae Others Six want to end the Reapers, the Dragon Kings, and take over the realm, and their leader is one of the most formidable enemies we've ever faced. The battle won't be easy, but with this strong, resilient mortal by my side and some help from our friends, it's a fight I'm more than willing to enter—as long as it means she's by my side. Forever.

Buy DARK ALPHA'S COMMAND today at
https://dgrant.co/3JebuKp

ABOUT THE AUTHOR

New York Times and *USA Today* bestselling author Donna Grant has been praised for her "totally addictive" and "unique and sensual" stories. She's written more than one hundred novels spanning multiple genres of romance including the bestselling Dark King series that features a thrilling combination of Dragon Kings, Druids, Fae, and immortal Highlanders who are dark, dangerous, and irresistible. She lives in Texas with her dog and a cat.

www.DonnaGrant.com
www.MotherofDragonsBooks.com

f facebook.com/AuthorDonnaGrant
instagram.com/dgauthor
BB bookbub.com/authors/donna-grant
a amazon.com/Donna-Grant/e/B00279DJGE
pinterest.com/donnagrant1

Printed in the USA
CPSIA information can be obtained
at www.ICGtesting.com
CBHW011024070724
11246CB00016B/1261